THE DEEP BLUE CRADLE

THE DEEP BLUE CRADLE

Peter Chambers

Chivers Press   •   Thorndike Press
Bath, England   Waterville, Maine USA

This Large Print edition is published by Chivers Press, England, and by Thorndike Press, USA.

Published in 2002 in the U.K. by arrangement with the author.

Published in 2002 in the U.S. by arrangement with Peter Chambers.

U.K. Hardcover ISBN 0–7540–7438–2 (Chivers Large Print)
U.K. Softcover ISBN 0–7540–7439–0 (Camden Large Print)
U.S. Softcover ISBN 0–7862–4504–2 (Nightingale Series Edition)

The text of this Large Print edition is unabridged.
Other aspects of the book may vary from the original edition.

Set in 16 pt. New Times Roman.

Printed in Great Britain on acid-free paper.

British Library Cataloguing in Publication Data available

Library of Congress Cataloging-in-Publication Data

Chambers, Peter, 1924–
    The deep blue cradle / by Peter Chambers.
      p.   cm.
    ISBN 0–7862–4504–2 (lg. print : sc : alk. paper)
    1. Ships—Fires and fire prevention—Fiction. 2. Large type
books. I. Title.
PR6066.H463 D44 2002
823'.914—dc21   2002074331

PROLOGUE

The harbor-master's office formed a small pool of yellow light on the near-deserted dock front. At one thirty in the morning all was still on the working section of Monkton Bay. The night was clear, with occasional drifting clouds, and there was little breeze to dispel the heat haze which had been hanging over the whole coastline for several weeks.

In the office, Ed Cartwright poured himself a mug of coffee, and completed the last of his obligatory one a.m. reports. Every hour throughout the shift he would be going through the same routine, making careful readings of temperature, wind pressures, visibility and the rest of it. Less than a mile away, the people in the Weather Bureau would be going through exactly the same motions, and sending the results through exactly the same channels. Cartwright groaned to himself, at the repetitive futility of it all. What did the authorities expect was going to happen? That the Weather Bureau people would invent some freak storm, or a tornado perhaps? Was that what he was doing here? Yes, that must be it. It was up to the harbor-master to maintain order, to ensure that the weather lunatics down at the Bureau did not get away with sudden sandstorms or unexpected icebergs.

1

Could throw the whole nation into a panic, that kind of thing.

'A flurry of unpredicted icebergs should hit the shore in an estimated thirty minutes,' he thought. 'These should engulf Los Angeles within the following two hours, after which there will be dense fog and a plague of locusts. Flight is hopeless.'

That would make a more interesting entry than all this boring stuff he'd written down. Rising, he went to the window, and stared across the moonlit bay, to where a fleet of small boats bobbed lazily on the gentle surface of the sea. A glare of light from the single storey buildings on the quayside announced that the hooley at the Monkton Bay Yacht Club was still in progress. They'd probably keep at it for another hour yet. Just his luck to be on duty that particular evening. An enthusiastic boatman himself, he would have enjoyed letting his hair down with some of those lunatics over there. Luck of the draw. His eyes moved along the bay, noting the occasional areas where people were swinging the night ordeal, like himself. Immigration, customs, dock police. Well no, leave out the police. They wouldn't be bored, whatever else they might be. This was no area for a policeman to fall asleep. Always plenty of work for those guys. The others would be making their last-minute preparations for this immigration vessel, due on the dawn tide.

What was that name again? He checked with the papers on his desk. That was it.

The S.S. *Newland Hope.*

*   *   *

The officer of the watch yawned, and stared out into the calm night. A few more hours, and another trip would go into the log. He'd call this one Operation Nursemaid.

The first alarm bell rang loud on the bridge.

'Fire, sir. No. 1 Hold.'

'Very well. Alert forward fire crews to proceed. Tell Mr. Aston I want a report from the site.'

'Fire sir, in the crew galley, aft.'

'What?'

'Fire sir, Lifeboat Davit Six.'

'What the hell is happening? Sound full alarm. All hands muster. Now. Now. Now. Captain. Captain. Bridge emergency, sir.'

There was no reply from the captain's cabin.

'Yeoman.'

'Sir.'

'I can't waste microphone time. Get the captain up here. On the double.'

'Sir.'

'Attention. This is the bridge. This is not a drill. Go to your fire stations at once. At once. Immediate. Repeat, this is not a drill.'

*   *   *

3

Jim Cowie sat at the control desk on the shiny, modern radio room in the yacht club. No expense had been spared to make that gleaming array of equipment the finest on the coast. Its only function was to keep contact with the members while they were afloat, but with a club like Monkton Bay, only the very best would suffice.

For a buff like Cowie, the radio room was a dream come true. He would sit, sometimes for hours at a stretch, and imagine himself the vital figure in some far-flung theater of war, relaying battle plans, last minute switches, warnings, emergencies. The reality was far more prosaic, except when the annual gala race meeting was in progress. Then the radio control came into its own, and Jim with it. For the entire three days he would not leave the club, but would remain hunched over the desk, eighteen hours without relief, a performance regarded with a mixture of scorn and reluctant admiration.

Tonight he had abandoned the revels as early as possible, escaping to his secret world, and was scanning the airwaves of the ocean-going Pacific traffic when the mayday came through from the S.S. *Newland Hope*. It was in plain language, loud and clear. And close. For a few moments he sat quite still, disbelief large in his mind, as this brutal reality pushed its way through fancies. Then he was up, out of his chair and racing out to the main clubroom.

It took him several minutes to get proper attention, and to blurt out his message. Then the deputy commodore, a grizzled ex-Navy veteran named Hawke, snapped.

'Distance from shore?'

'Four miles sir.'

Hawke was the kind of man you called 'sir', civilian or not. He rose now, amid silence, and stared coldly around at the expectant faces.

'We have a mayday, gentlemen. You heard Jim Cowie. An immigration ship is on fire, four miles off the coast. There are two thousand souls aboard, eighteen hundred of them babies in arms. I need fast power-boats, and sailors. No drunks, no sightseers. I shall spend exactly five minutes checking with the harbor-master.' He looked at his watch, and held it up, tapping at the glass. 'In eight minutes, I want the sailors ready to leave, and the drunks out of the way. I suggest you spend the time under cold showers. Mr. Cowie, you will come with me, please.'

The two men strode out. There was a stunned silence, then a voice shouted,

'You heard the man. Let's get to it.'

*   *   *

The telephone in the immigration office rang four times before anyone answered.

'Immigration.'

5

'This is Ed Cartwright,' said an urgent voice.

'Who?'

'Acting harbor-master.

'Oh. What is it, Ed?'

The listening man suddenly found himself standing upright.

'You're sure about this? What rescue stuff have you sent out?'

'Two fire-tugs is all I have. There are fishing boats out there, but it'll be an hour before the nearest one can rendezvous. The coastguards are on the way, but they couldn't take off more than a couple of dozen people. What can you do?'

'All we have here is one launch. And the chopper. They'll be on their way as soon as I can muster crews.'

'Right. I won't keep you.'

The immigration man left the room on the double.

*   *   *

The two smaller fires were brought quickly under control, but No. 1 Hold was ablaze, and sweating crewmen were throwing in every device to contain it.

On the bridge, First Officer Arch Winters watched the thick black smoke as it billowed upwards, enveloping the half-lit figures of the firefighters. Everything was going to be all right, he breathed. The fire-tugs would

6

rendezvous in another ten minutes. There was no question of losing the ship, the nightmare of every sailor. If they'd been a further fifty miles from shore—another thirty—well, they weren't, and thank God for it. Mind you, there would be one hell of a row after all this. Fires do not get started simultaneously in three different places. There was sabotage here, no doubt of it, and the months to come would be an endless time of enquiries, investigations and commissions. As for the captain, well. Unconsciously, Winters shrugged. You just never knew about people. It was unthinkable that a man like him would be drunk at sea. On duty, off duty, any time. In thirty years sea-time, Winters could not recall having served under a more efficient or correct sailor. But there was no escaping the facts. The captain had been unfit to command, impossible even to rouse properly, and no amount of loyalty or evasion would hide that unpalatable truth from the investigators. He realised there was a new presence on the bridge.

'Doctor Freeman, what are you doing here? Please leave the bridge at once.'

'Mr. Winters, you must abandon ship.'

The words were terse, flung at him like chips of ice.

The acting captain looked at the wild-eyed figure in amazement.

'Abandon ship?' he echoed. 'You seem to have lost control, doctor. There is no danger

7

here. My men have the main fire under control. In ten minutes the tugs will be here, and—'

'That will be too late. You are wrong about the danger. Look at it, man. I've already treated two of your men, suffering from that smoke.'

Winters clucked impatiently.

'I know it's unpleasant, but you don't abandon ship just because a few people cough. Go away, sir.'

'I will not go away. A man can absorb a certain amount of that stuff, but there are eighteen hundred babies on this ship. Do you know how much of that smoke it takes to kill one? A fistful, Mr. Winters. Those babies have to be put to sea, away from this.'

'You're exaggerating, doctor. We're all under a strain here.'

'I am telling you, in my official capacity, and in front of these witnesses here, that fifty to seventy per cent of those babies will die if we don't get them away from that smoke. A thousand lives, Mr. Winters. Probably more. Lower your boats.'

Winters hesitated. Grim-faced crewmen watched the scene. They didn't know whether the doctor was making an unnecessary fuss, but they did know the dilemma that was raging in the first officer's mind. They also knew the first rule of the sea. Human life comes first.

'Captain, sir.'

8

'What is it, helmsman?'

'Away to starboard sir. A phenomenon. Looks like fireflies.'

Fireflies? Winters swung his night-glasses along the line of the helmsman's pointing finger. It wasn't a phenomenon. It was a cluster of bobbing lights, speeding towards the ship. Small craft.

'What the devil—'

'Radio message, sir.'

He took the flimsy, and stared at it.

'Mr. Aston.'

'Sir.'

'There is a flotilla of small boats approaching to give assistance, if we need it. We do not. There is no need to abandon this ship, and no such order will be given. However, in view of the possible health hazard, I am authorising the premature disembarkation of all children passengers. You will take charge of the operation Mr. Aston. Doctor Freeman, you will please place yourself and your staff under Mr. Aston's directions. Signalman.'

'Sir.'

'Radio message to leader of small boats. Message begins—'

Aston and the doctor left the bridge on the run.

*   *   *

9

The helicopter swung steadily above the scene, the dark, oily smoke-cloud split by occasional tongues of red and yellow flame, and the lights of the yacht club launches as they rushed towards the disaster.

'What do those guys think they're doing?' wondered the pilot.

The immigration officer grunted.

'Search me. The ship's captain has confirmed the fire is under control. Can we go further in, and get a close-up?'

The pilot shook his head.

'Guess not. This is as close as baby and I go to a fire at sea. A sudden shift of wind and we can be in a heap of trouble. Instead of just watching a fire, we could be part of it.'

'What about the loud-hailer?'

'It may look like a silent movie from up here, but down there all hell is breaking loose. They'd never hear us.'

'So we just watch?'

'That's it.'

*   *   *

In one of the leading boats, Cal Goldsmith shouted as another great spray enveloped him. Whatever state he may have been in twenty minutes ago, he was stone cold sober now. Make that cold, wet sober, he amended. His companion nudged him, pointing.

'Who's that over there?'

10

Goldsmith stared out to port. Then he snorted.

'That's the *Flying Revenge,* you oughta know that.'

'No, no,' insisted the other. 'Beyond the *Revenge.* Looks like a Talisman class, very high in the water.'

Goldsmith kept on staring, but finally shook his head.

'Too much of this wet static around,' he grumbled. 'Anyway, what does it matter, as long as he's here?'

'Yeah. I guess that's right.'

*   *   *

The first of the rescue launches nosed against the quayside. Doctor Freeman jumped clear, and ran to meet the approaching watchers. One of them said,

'Doctor Freeman, isn't it? I'm from Ad Hoc. I have a qualified nurse with me, and two trained orderlies on the way.'

'Thank God,' mumbled Freeman. 'Can you start to get some real medical shape to this thing? I'm going to have to do battle with the authorities. The Lord alone knows how many laws we're breaking.'

'Leave it with me, doctor. Nurse.'

The doctor turned thankfully away, to the first of the port officials.

11

        *   *   *

Arch Winters watched gratefully as the great spouts rose from the fire-tugs and located their target. It was all over bar the shouting. He grinned to himself ruefully, as the old saying came into his head. Whoever dreamed that one up must have known what was going to happen this balmy night on the S.S. *Newland Hope*.

The shouting after this episode would be a long time a-dying.

CHAPTER ONE

The indicator light in the hi-speed elevator clicked over to 'P' and the white doors slid soundlessly open. 'P' was for penthouse, and I was now at the pinnacle of the steel and concrete finger that jabbed upwards into the Monkton City sky. A quick peek at the floor told me my stomach wasn't there. It was probably still around the thirty-eighth storey, or maybe the twenty-fifth. I knew from experience that stomachs don't travel upwards as fast as the rest of a man. It would be along later.

The hallway was small, dominated by the plain oak door of the penthouse suite. There was no way a man could get confused. You had

12

two choices. Either you went into the oak door, or you got back in the elevator. I looked around for something to press or bang. Then the door opened, and a man stood looking at me. He was a tall, good-looking character, in his late twenties. Very neat in the pressed blue alpaca, with the silk shirt and the soft wool tie. The kind of appearance that makes you wonder whether you shaved close enough today.

'I was looking for the buzzer.'

'There isn't one,' he told me. The voice was the predictable mellow tone that would go with the rest of him. 'When the elevator arrives at this level, the door-chimes ring automatically.'

They would.

'Name is Preston,' I told him. 'I'm here to see a Mr. Shoemaker. Mr. Otto P. Shoemaker.'

There was just a tiny glint in his eye as he replied.

'Yes. Right this way, Mr. Preston.'

I hadn't bothered to ask whether his name was Shoemaker. It wouldn't be. He led me through into a room that was marginally smaller than the Hollywood Bowl, and left me standing there.

'Mr. Shoemaker will be right along.'

The room seemed to be divided into sections, judging by the way the furniture was laid out. Almost as though there were about five different rooms, and somebody had

13

removed the partitioning walls. What would a man do, left to himself in a room like that? It was no place to spend a cosy evening, that was for sure. A small set of Chinese figures on an ivory table caught my eye. I was looking at them, but not daring to touch, when a voice said.

'Nice, aren't they?'

I took my first look at him. At least, I imagined it was to be my first look. When I saw the famous face, I said,

'You're—'

'Otto P. Shoemaker,' he replied firmly.

'Maybe the papers have been misleading me all these years. Still, I guess a man should know his own name.'

'Shoemaker,' he nodded.

And so I referred to him by that name throughout the whole affair.

I knew he had to be close to sixty years old, but it was hard to accept. He was still as upright as the day he won the Army–Navy game practically single-handed. Still the same fearless, look-em-in-the-eye character who'd been the natural choice to lead the Victory Parade in Monkton after World War Two. The man who'd been the people's choice all his life, and who was now heading for that little place in Washington which is painted white. That is, if you can believe what you read in the papers. But then, they didn't even know his name was Shoemaker.

'They tell me you drink scotch whisky,' he boomed. 'There's a gallon or two of Old Angus somewhere around here.'

'I'd offer to help find it,' I replied. 'But I didn't think to bring a compass.'

'Ha. Good. Don't worry about it. I know the way.'

Soon, I was holding a chunky tumbler which made a familiar clinking sound as the ice banged around. My host had a glass too, but his mixture was thinner.

'Let's sit down, and talk a minute.'

He sprawled into a large armchair in what seemed to be the lounging section. I parked nearby, and we looked each other over.

'I hear you're a Marx Brothers nut,' he threw.

I shrugged.

'Isn't everybody? It isn't a full-time occupation, by the way.'

'Ever meet him? Groucho?'

'No. I never did.'

He smiled reminiscently.

'I met him a couple of times. What a man. Do you know, I invited him to a big party dinner one time. One of my great treasures is the letter he wrote back. He said, let me think, he already had a professional engagement. There was going to be a gala opening of an outdoor hotdog stand. Naturally an ambitious guy couldn't turn down an opportunity like that, not to mention the fifteen dollar fee. And certainly not to sit around chewing stogies with a bunch of ward-heelers. The letter is in my desk out at the house. I'll show it to you some time, when you're out visiting.'

'I'd like to see it,' I grinned. 'Was it signed Shoemaker?'

He looked guilty, like a kid caught at the ice-box.

'Come to mention it, I believe it was.'

The man would talk when he was ready. I was happy with things as they were. Down below, the world was full of hot dusty streets and the streets were full of hot, dusty people. Up here, it was cool and refreshing. People sat around drinking good whisky, and talking about Groucho. Civilised.

He set down his glass. The drink-level had scarcely altered.

'You're wondering, why you?' he challenged.

'It had crossed my mind.'

The handsome head nodded.

'Naturally, I don't have to blow any trumpets. You know who I am. I'm a big man, big in every sense of the word. Money-wise, politics-wise, you name it. Anything I want done, anything at all, there's a hundred guys out there who'll bust a leg to be first in line. So why you?'

I heaved my shoulders, and waited.

'If it's dirty, I have guys called political aides. If it's investigation, I can hire the biggest

16

outfit in the country. But there are problems, and the main one is security. Before I can expect a man to do something, I have to tell him what it is. He may keep records, a diary, some kind of note. And he has to account for his time. Besides which, for every man out there who's rooting for me, there are two others who'd seize any opportunity to bring me down.'

He squinted at me, to see if I wanted to argue. I didn't.

'I need a man to do something for me which is strictly personal, and remains that way. A pushy, hard-nosed kind of man, who won't burst out crying if somebody slaps his wrist. An obstinate man, a solo operator. Reliable. You're it.'

'It sounds very mysterious,' I suggested.

'That's just it. It's a very simple matter really. If I was Joe Citizen, nobody would give it a second thought. But, being who I am, it could be made into something. Something big and important.'

I knew what he meant. If this man sneezed, it was flashed across the nation. 'Candidate's health in doubt'. Whatever this little errand might be, the opposition could certainly turn it into hay.

'Well, Mr. Shoemaker, I'd have to hear the story before I agreed to do anything.'

'Yes. But even if you turn me down, it still remains a matter between the two of us.

Right?'

'You got it. How about your assistant out there, the one who let me in?'

The great man snorted.

'Assistant? That's rich. The only assistance I get from him is that he helps spend my money. My son, Andrew. He doesn't know why you're here. He doesn't play politics. He plays tennis.'

In uttering the last word, he betrayed all the traditional contempt of the contact-sportsman. I stared into my disappearing drink, and made no comment.

'I have another son, Jeff. He's away in the Navy.'

'I know,' I contributed. 'I read about that fire on his ship last year. He did all right.'

'Jeff is O.K.,' said his father positively. 'But it isn't about the boys I want to talk. It's my daughter, Angie. You probably read about her last year, too. And the year before that. Any year.'

There was resignation and despair in the words, and on his face. But there was love, as well. Love and defiance. Angie Proctor—it was the title she retained from the second failed marriage—was a name to conjure with by anybody's standards. I nodded.

'She gets a lot of press. I dare say a lot of it is exaggerated.'

'A lot of it?' he queried. 'You don't think it's all blown up, then?'

'No, I don't,' I told him frankly. 'These

18

stories lose nothing in the telling, because she's your daughter—but they're not invented. Angela Proctor is a lady who—er—makes news.'

Again that quizzical look.

'You don't mince your words, do you?'

'Mr. Shoemaker,' I replied evenly, 'you want your words minced, there's a hundred guys out there who'll break a leg to be first at the mince machine. You said so yourself. Do I push the buzzer?'

He flapped a resigned hand.

'Don't be so touchy. Anyway, it's true. Angie has one hell of a knack for putting her feet wrong.'

'And she's about to do it again, and that's why I'm here,' I finished.

Shoemaker sat well back in the chair, his drink forgotten, and stared at the ceiling.

'I don't know what she's about to do,' he admitted, 'but then, I never have. Not since she was twelve years old.'

He went on talking, remembering.

Angela had been welcomed into the world with considerable delight. Her two brothers were already on the scene, a good healthy pair of tumbling roustabouts. The arrival of a golden-haired girl seemed to complete the family. To the boys, she was a curiosity, a creature to be handled with some care, and treated with reserve. Everyone noted this with approval, because that was the way things

19

should be. Everyone, that is, but Angela. She didn't care to have her hair curled, and sit around wearing pretty clothes. The real world was outside, where the boys were. The world where you climbed trees, and got into fights, and took the skin off your knees at regular intervals. So out she went, and the people of that world, sceptical at first, soon learned that the angel with the fair hair was in fact as rough as any of them, and tougher than most. While her contemporaries were taking their first lessons on violin or piano, Angela was learning how to skin a jackrabbit, so that the pelt came off all of a piece. When they began to learn French, she was acquiring the curious art of conversing in that mixture of English, low Yiddish, and jazz talk and underworld terms which is the patois of the streets and the poolroom.

It was decided that Angela would be better off away from home, at a school where she would learn to Become a Lady. The school stuck to its task for almost two years, before they finally gave up and sent her home. It was the first time the Press had any reason to notice this daughter of a famous father, and they printed small items about her inability to adapt to the close environment of a boarding establishment. The family did not trouble the newspapers about the teacher who had suffered a nervous breakdown, and of course, the business of the fire-ravaged gymnasium was quickly dealt with by a handsome financial settlement. Even Angela seemed to have learned something from the experience, and contrived to avoid any major disasters after that. The family finally felt confident enough, when she was sixteen, to send her to finishing school in Switzerland. That lasted three months, ending abruptly when she led a party of girls on an expedition. This took place at three o'clock one morning, and the object of the expedition was to scale the walls of a nearby monastery, which was achieved with disastrous effect.

At seventeen, she took off with a trombone-player, and it was five weeks before an army of private investigators tracked her to a joint in Philadelphia, where she was singing in front of a five-piece band, on a sandwiches and coffee basis. By this time, the Press were alive to the fact that this girl was a news item, and subsequent escapades were recorded, more or less accurately.

When she married Alvin Jefferson Hunter the Third, everyone gave a great sigh of relief. It had all come good in the end, and two famous families had been united. Unfortunately, Alvin did not measure up to requirements. His enormous grasp of financial matters, of Wall Street, banking, and overseas investment, could not compensate for his ignorance in such important areas as baseball batting averages, the names of the Original

21

Mound City Blue Blowers, and where to locate the most authentic Mexican tamale joint. Alvin lasted almost eighteen months, despite these shortcomings, before Angela did something rather lacking in originality, by her standards. It is almost a tradition that a certain percentage of the heiress types along the southernmost end of the West Coast will sooner or later disappear with a bullfighter. For once, Angela stuck to tradition, and was hauled, struggling, from some third rate arena down near La Paz.

She went to Europe, and nothing more was heard of her for a while. Over there, a pretty girl in jeans is just one of an army, and there is more regard for anonymity. If Angela didn't insist on broadcasting her real identity, it was unlikely to be discovered. Whatever she did during that period remained mercifully unknown. Until the Marseilles incident, that is.

It appears that she was living in some kind of commune at the time, scraping a living of sorts from directing tourists, who spoke no French, to local places of historic interest. In the evenings, she would conduct them on guided tours of places where the entertainment was also historic, but where notions of the distribution of wealth were strictly late twentieth century. There was one particular wharf-rat who decided her talents and looks were being wasted on these excursions. He would take her under his protection, and put her to work. He began to explain this to her one night, with his fists, which is the traditional method of recruitment. Unfortunately for him, he didn't know Angela. Since the man was bigger and heavier, it was only fair that she should enlist the aid of a three foot crowbar which was lying around. The resultant disturbance was so bad, that even the Marseilles police had to take an interest, and anyone who knows the neighbourhood can imagine the extent of the carnage necessary before that happens.

It was to be a disturbed night for a whole flock of people, officials of all kinds, attorneys, bank managers, embassy staff. Angela knew she was in real trouble this time, with a possible long term of years in a French penitentiary ahead of her. She had never been one to ask for help from her family, but this time she hollered murder. One month later, when it was confirmed that her assailant was not going to die, and after much legal and political wrangling, Angela was despatched from French soil by hard-eyed men who had made certain she would never re-enter that great country.

This time, she really had taken a beating. She needed rest and quiet, a chance to reflect. This she was given, under the kindly and expert tutelage of one Doctor Edwin Proctor. He was a gentle and civilised man, a forty-year-old widower, and Angela's response to

23

the treatment was to marry the guy. That had been two years ago, and she was twenty-three at the time. It lasted six months, then she moved out.

I didn't know whether there was a second divorce, only that she still used the doctor's name. My prospective client finished speaking.

'I imagine you knew most of that, Mr. Preston?'

'Most,' I admitted. 'But it saves time, hearing it your way. I've been getting it in segments, over the years, well padded out with a lot of lurid details.'

'And florid imaginings,' he supplemented.

'That too, I don't doubt. Anyway,' I added hopefully, 'there's been nothing about Mrs. Proctor for quite some time now.'

He nodded.

'I know. In a way, that's one of the things that bothers me. When you have a hell-cat on your hands, you know where you stand. You're on guard all the time. Watching, waiting, every minute. When she turns into a hearthrug cat, you get suspicious, irritable. It's unnatural.'

I don't know too much about cats, so I kept quiet.

'Angie seems to have resigned from the trouble spots, Mr. Preston. She goes to work every day and works eight hours, often more. Maybe she plays a little hell in the evenings, I wouldn't know. But if she does, she keeps very quiet about it.'

24

'We all get to learn discretion in the end.'

He made a noise that sounded like 'harrumph'.

'This job she has,' I probed. 'Is it necessary? I mean, obviously I know nothing about her affairs, but I'm surprised she has to work.'

He offered a box of thin brown cigars, and we lit them. They were soft, and unexciting, but the smoke smelled good.

'Let me tell you about the job. Oh, and you're right. She doesn't need to work, not in any financial sense. My daughter is a wealthy woman in her own right. But I think she does need a job, this particular job anyway, for moral or social reasons. I'll need to explain that.'

I waved the cigar to indicate that some explanation would be welcome.

'As you are well aware, as we are all of us aware, the recent wars in the East have created enormous displacement problems for hundreds of thousands of people. At government level, we are doing everything in our power to alleviate the suffering. Some people say we do too much.'

'Some say we don't do enough,' I countered.

He smiled sadly.

'Well, there's a three-day conversation you and I could have at some future time. Right now, let's just agree there is a problem, and it has to be dealt with. Now, in addition to the work which is being done officially, there are a number of private organisations involved. Most of them are sincere, soundly-based, and effective. There are one or two crackpots, naturally, but there always are. A number of these societies deal solely with the children who've been displaced. Angela works for one of these. Aid for Displaced, Homeless Orphan Children. You've heard of it, I imagine? People usually refer to it by the initials only. They call it Ad-Hoc.'

Until he used the abbreviation, I'd been floundering. But Ad-Hoc rang a bell.

'Why sure,' I agreed. 'Wasn't there a big charity concert over in L.A. a week or two back? Lot of star names, Hollywood people and so forth?'

'That's the one. Oh, the organisation is substantial enough. I'm fairly confident of that. Not one of the lunatic fringe I was talking about. Not by any means.'

'Then I would suggest your daughter is doing a good job.'

'Right,' he assented. 'Me too. But you know how these things can become distorted, when you're a politician. There are a lot of people in this country, both in power and out, who say we ought to be cutting back on our aid to foreigners, not increasing it.'

'But Ad-Hoc doesn't rely on help from government sources,' I protested. 'It's privately-run. I don't see the connection.'

The ash on his cigar was over an inch long.

He moved it carefully through the air until he could safely tap it into a silver tray.

Softly he said,

'It's easy to see you're not a political man. As I've said, this aid business is a political hot potato. By allowing my own daughter to spend her life working for these children, I would seem to be supporting the view that the government allocations are inadequate. If they were, there would be no demand for these voluntary efforts. Now do you see?'

I thought about it.

'I think you're making too much of it. Your daughter is a free woman, she doesn't need your permission about where she works. She doesn't even use your name.'

'You're being naive,' he accused. 'What I make of the situation is irrelevant. It's what other people make of it, people who are not even concerned with the truth. I can be made to look bad. However, that is not the main point. This outfit, Ad-Hoc, has not been cleared one hundred per cent, politically. Some of these societies, for all the good work they do, are basically acting against the best interests of this country. Using this fireproof cover as a means of gaining control over our new immigrant populations. It's all very insidious, very hard to prove, but it's there.'

'Are you saying Ad-Hoc is sponsored by the Reds?'

'No, of course not. But all these

27

organisations are vetted by our security people, with this very possibility in mind. Most of them are given a clean bill. I get to know which ones they are. Ad-Hoc has not been listed so far.'

'What do our—um—security people have against Ad-Hoc?'

'Ah.'

He sighed, and took a slow puff before replying.

'That's the trouble. As I said, I am told which organisation is clean. That's all I'm told. No one will give reasons as to why a particular society has not been given clearance. It is simply described as "Not Cleared".'

'But that's the same as not giving a man a trial,' I protested.

'It's worse than that. It's like saying a man has not been proven innocent. He isn't guilty, and no one's saying he is. He isn't even accused of anything. He simply has not been proven innocent.'

'Wow. Next thing you know, we'll be burning witches.'

He made a grimace.

'I can see you are beginning to get the idea. How's the drink, by the way? You ready for another?'

'No thanks, Mr—Shoemaker. This is fine. So we have your daughter working for this charitable outfit, which has not been given security blessing. What do you want me to do?'

He stood up, smoothing out his clothes. Then he placed his hands behind his back, very much the candidate.

'Find out what she's up to. How deeply she is involved with these people. Find out what she does with her evenings, weekends. Whom she sees, mixes with. Does she have two lives, like most people? A working life, which ends at five or six o'clock, and then a social life with different backgrounds, a different set of people? Or do the two merge, the work and the private life?'

I swallowed the last of my scotch. We were getting near the end of the interview.

'I think I'm getting your drift. These children need help, and your daughter is doing what she can. That's fine. But if she spends her free time with the organisers, then there could be something more to it than the promptings of her social conscience. Something stronger, perhaps even ideological. Is that it?'

'It's not so far-fetched, is it? Mr. Preston, these next three months are of vital importance to me, to my whole career. If there are any bad apples in my barrel, I had better know about it before anyone else does.'

He'd be good, I reflected. An impressive man to have standing on that platform. The way he looked at that moment, he could be assured of anybody's vote.

'It's a hell of an assignment,' I muttered, half to myself.

'Yes, it is,' he agreed. 'It's a hell of a responsibility, too. If you do it wrong you could cause me a severe setback. Well, are you going to give it a try?'

Before replying, I got to my feet. He was an inch and a half taller, strain as I might.

'It would have to be just between us,' I demurred. 'You, and me. No middleman, no secretaries. As you said, you have powerful enemies. I don't need them out prowling for me. They could put me out of business in twenty-four hours.'

'Quicker,' he confirmed. 'Well?'

'I'd need a lot of details, addresses, telephone numbers—'

'—All here. In this envelope. Including where you can contact Mr. Shoemaker. At certain times, that is.'

I hesitated, then took the white envelope, tapped it against my cheek, and pushed it inside my jacket. He watched with approval.

'I guess I took the job, didn't I, Mr. Shoemaker?'

'I guess you did, Mr. Preston.'

'No, wait a minute. Preston won't do.' I dug around in the recesses of memory. There was a desk drawer, with a frypan cooking inside. A door with a dummy's arm, holding phoney telegrams. On the outer door was a legend, and I finally brought it into focus. 'Mr. Shoemaker, for this exercise, my name will be Flywheel.'

30

Two could play at that game.

CHAPTER TWO

There is a part of town where the business
section merges gently with the funny business
section. Where the brokerage houses, the main
banks, the investment companies and the big
shippers begin to make way for the smaller
business premises, and these in turn to the
one-man operations, and then the operators.

The building housing Aid for Displaced and
Homeless Orphan Children was situated
neatly on the dividing line. Not close enough
to be confused with the old-established outfits,
but not far enough away to draw suspicion.

Officially, the office hours ended at five
p.m. It was now five twenty, and only two cars
remained in the reserved slots. One of these
was the distinctive red M.G. which was listed
to one Mrs. Angela Proctor. The other was a
dusty six-year-old Ford, which would have
scared off any prospective investor if it had
been parked half a block further back. I sat
across the street, watching the front of the
building and waiting. Shortly before five thirty,
the glass doors slid aside, and out stepped a
tall, fair-haired woman. She would have
attracted my attention whether I'd been
waiting for her or not. The long, rangy body

was covered by a white linen skirt, topped off with a vertical-striped smock affair, head held upright as she walked out, with the free-striding confidence of the very beautiful, or the very rich. Or both.

Beside her scuttled a pale, gangling man about thirty years old. He was talking rapidly, as though he knew he had to get it all said before she reached the car. She appeared to pay him no attention whatever, but kept heading for the M.G. As she was about to climb in, he put a hand on her arm, still talking. She paid attention then. Turning towards him, she said something, not more than a couple of words. Then, with fingers extended in the way women normally reserve for removing a dead mouse, she lifted his hand with distaste from her arm, and dropped it, as into a garbage can. The man went even paler, and stopped talking for a moment.

There was a throaty roar from the powerful engine. Angela Proctor swept a quick glance around at the street, then backed quickly out, slipped into forward gear, and drove away. The man stared after her, shrugged, and went back inside. I was already moving behind the sport car, keeping three cars between us in the evening business traffic. To my surprise, we didn't go very far. After a couple of blocks, my red target edged to the kerb, and stopped. I drove past, to the first available parking spot, and watched in the rear-view mirror.

Angela Proctor got out of the car, and walked over to a row of pay-phones. They were all busy, and she stood waiting, paying no attention to the glances from the male section of the passing foot traffic. A man stepped out from one of the booths, and she went quickly inside. I was tempted to go and get close, to see if there was any chance of finding out who she was talking to, but I sat tight. If the lady was going to get a look at me, it ought to be later, rather than sooner. The phone-call intrigued me. She'd just left an office, with presumably half a dozen telephones at least. So, this call was one she didn't want overheard. At least, not by the people she worked with. She was too far away for me to distinguish facial expressions. After less than a minute, she emerged and got back into the car. As she drove past me, I slid down in the seat, and shielded my eyes with my right hand. Then I took up the chase again. Not that it was much of a chase. Angela Proctor drove with skill and care, and was not out to break any land-speed records.

Within five minutes we were clear of the town, and it began to look as if she was heading home. Sure enough, four miles outside the limits, she turned into that expensive, sheltered bungalow village called Roseland Drive. This is an exclusive development of half-acre plots, each building designed to the owner's specification, and strictly no two alike. The area had not been levelled, the original contours being retained deliberately. The result was that the houses were sometimes sheltered in small ravines, sometimes dominating a small hill, and yet again some appeared to be clinging to a slope. Each place was a discovery in its own right, and each discovery a new pleasure. It was an area of lush vegetation and exotic tropic growths, thanks to the continuous whirling sprinklers, and the quieter whirr of the high credit ratings.

Ex-Mrs. Proctor lived halfway along the wide tree-lined avenue, and I watched the M.G. mount the rather steep incline of the driveway. Then I turned the car around and went back to the main highway to think. In plenty of locations I could have parked in the road and kept an eye on the house. In Roseland Drive, a parked unknown car would quickly be the focus of suspicious interest. I would either be tackled by a houseowner, or find myself talking to the highway patrol. There was nothing lost as it happened, because the road was a cul-de-sac, and if the lady decided to go out visiting, she would have to come my way again. I loosened my tie, and settled down, to run over in my mind the stuff her father had been telling me a few hours earlier. That phonecall kept intruding. O.K., so she didn't want to make a call from the office. That was understandable. But why not leave it until she got home? I only had two answers to that. One was that she feared her home telephone might be tapped. A remote idea, that, but not impossible. The other was that there was somebody in the house, whom she did not wish to overhear the conversation. There had been no other car parked outside, but that did not necessarily prove there was no one else in the house. I chewed around on both explanations, and didn't really like either one.

It was six fifteen. I tried to imagine what a working girl would be doing, at the end of a hot day. She'd probably mix herself a drink, and then take a shower, for openers. Or maybe there'd be a pool at the back of the house. I hadn't been able to tell from where I was parked. Yes, that's what she'd be doing. Splashing around in some cool water, with an iced drink waiting in the shade of a small, pool-side table. I licked at some sweat that ran down off my upper lip, and stared morosely at the unending desert scrub.

The minutes ticked away. Occasionally, a car would separate from the highway stream and turn into Roseland Drive. I watched each one with care, until it turned into one of the driveways, then lost interest. Just before seven, a large white Packard appeared. The driver was a heavy-set man, fortyish, with a face that seemed vaguely familiar. I waited for him to select some other address, but he didn't.

35

Instead, he rolled up that same incline, and parked behind the M.G. By the time I'd started up, and followed him down the road, he'd already been admitted to the house. I drove past to the end, reversed around, and came back again, making a careful note of the license plate. Then I went back to my private piece of desert again, and waited. If the man in the Packard was going to escort the lady somewhere, I ought to know within about thirty minutes. That would give him time to have a drink, and her time to decide her dress was all wrong, and change it. If, on the other hand, they were going to settle down to a heavy session of Mah-Jong, or whatever it is guys settle down to with twenty-five year old hellcats these days, it could be longer. Much longer. My job was to find out the girl's social life, not to peep through keyholes. If the guy was still there after forty minutes, I would call it a night.

Twenty minutes later, I had arrived at the stage of planning some kind of an evening for myself, when the white Packard suddenly reappeared. The same man was driving, and although the sun was slanted across his windshield, I didn't have to be a hot shot detective to work out who was sitting beside him. They turned away from Monkton, and headed inland. That meant my back was towards them, so once again she didn't get a look at my face, even if she was interested.

36

Traffic by now was thin on the straight flat highway. I could easily afford to let them stay a quarter mile ahead, without any real danger of losing them. Six miles along, the road took a wide right-hand sweep to negotiate the foot of a small mountain. At the far end of this was situated a dine and dance joint called Buck's Rancho. Maybe my people were just slipping in there for some refreshment. I took the bend with care, slowing as I approached the turn-off to the eaterie, and was just in time to see the familiar white shape swinging in a half-circle in the parking lot.

There was a fancy wood-pole gateway, with a cow's skull at either end of the top crossing pole. The neon lighting of the sign still looked pale against the evening sun, but it would come into its own in another hour.

I took it easy up the rutted track towards the sprawling single storey group of buildings. The Rancho was a recent venture, and I hadn't yet had any need to head out in this direction. The place had opened up in a fair cloud of ballyhoo, with its two pound steaks and genuine cowhand trimmings. There would be western dancing, and if you felt like a canter on a genuine cowpony, that could be arranged too. I parked well clear of the Packard, and walked past the stables to the main entrance, climbing three broad wooden steps to a verandah. Outside the swing-to doors, a man sat back on a plain chair, stetson tilted over his eyes. He wore a rough woollen shirt, and buckskin pants, with worn leather boots and a heavy gunbelt. As a change from the usual fancy-dan dude-ranch cowboy, he looked like the real thing, right down to the worm-handled sixgun that hung at his side. His hands were busy with a piece of wood and a knife, as he whittled industriously away, watching me beneath the brim of the dark hat.

'Howdy,' he greeted.

He was certainly the most original doorkeeper I'd encountered.

'Evening,' I replied. 'Been a hot day.'

'Ain't it, though. Everything is cool inside, stranger.'

He dropped his eyes, and I nodded, pushing open the doors. There was a semi-circular entrance hall with three doors, then a wide open entrance into the bar. The first door carried the legend 'Foreman's Office'. The other two were marked respectively with a six-gun and a parasol, so that there'd be no misunderstanding about who went where. Evidently they weren't expecting Calamity Jane. I stood at the bar entrance, taking in the scene. There was a long black-topped bar to one side, and wooden chairs and tables scattered around. Despite the early hour, there were quite a few customers on view, and white-aproned waiters moved around with trays of drinks. At the far side was a handwritten sign 'Ma Kelly's Eats'. I walked across the floor,

38

and peeked in. Angela Proctor and the Packard owner were poring over menus. I went over to the bar, and a man with a slick of black hair glued to his forehead wiped needlessly at the immaculate surface.

'What's your pleasure?'

I asked for beer, and was soon staring at six inches of foaming suds. If a man didn't feel up to Ma Kelly's Eats, he could order a quick snack in the bar. There were some frightening descriptions of what was on offer, but I noticed that most of the grub looked very familiar when one of the hungry travellers summoned up the courage to order it. It occurred to me that this might be my only opportunity to eat that evening. I beckoned the bartender over.

'What's a Round-Up Special?' I demanded.

'Kind of a sandwich,' he explained. 'Like a slice of bread, then a good thick hunk of bacon. On top of that there's a whole flock of beans. They got a special sauce, like a mixture of mustard and chilli, and they kind of pour this over the whole shebang. It's very popular. At two and a half bucks, what can you lose?'

Just the temporary stoppage of my digestive system, by the sound of it.

'I'll try one of those.'

'You got it.'

He waved towards a waiter, making movements with his hands, then said,

'About two minutes. You wanta pay me now?'

I paid him now, and got some more foam on my nose while I waited. Over in one corner, a girl had set a chair on a small platform, and she sat down with a Spanish guitar cradled in her arms. There was no microphone, and the guitar was not wired. After a few plucks at the strings, she began to sing Moonlight in the Rockies, more or less to herself. No one paid any attention, and she didn't seem to expect it, but I found the gentle sound pleasant and relaxing. Not that I could hear very well, especially with the guy sitting next to me, who kept talking to his companion in an overloud voice.

'You like the song, mister?'

The bar jockey leaned nearby, listening.

'What I can hear of it,' I grumbled. 'Why don't those people keep quiet and listen?'

He chuckled.

'It's always the same, this time of night. In a couple of hours from now, she'll have all these bums—sorry, customers—she'll have 'em all crying in their beer. Home Sweet Home, Moonlight Bay, you wait. That's Annie Farmer, that's who that is. Has her own show, Friday nights, on MCR.'

I looked at her again, hearing the name. She certainly looked like the cowboy's dream of home. And not just the cowboy's.

'Here comes your sandwich.'

I turned to see the waiter getting close. The loudmouth behind me laughed boisterously.

'I'm telling you, that fish was this big.'

As he said 'this', he flung out his arms. The waiter was too close to dodge. Up went the tray, and down came the Round-Up Special. The world became a forest of beans and gravy, all of it headed for me. I flung up an arm, but nothing was going to halt that particular deluge. My sleeve took most of it, but the front of my jacket came in for its share. For a second I saw a frozen tableau. The shocked faces of the bartender and the waiter, the horrified look of the man who'd done the damage.

'Jeez, I'm sorry buddy. I sure didn't mean—'

'Forget it, forget it,' I muttered, dabbing beans off here and there and other places.

'What's the trouble here? Oh.'

A tall cowboy had appeared from nowhere, asking and answering his own question in the same breath.

'Listen, this is all my fault,' said Loudmouth. 'I'll have to pay the damage. I sure am sorry.'

One thing I didn't want was to be the centre of attention. At least Annie Farmer had the sense to go on singing.

'If I could just get the jacket wiped over,' I muttered. 'Could somebody lend me a cloth?'

The cowboy took me by the arm.

'Just come this way sir, and we'll get you fixed up in a second.'

I followed him into the kitchen and stripped off my jacket.

'Louis, do what you can with this,' snapped

41

my guide.

Louis didn't do at all badly, in the circumstances. He got most of the stain out, but chilli and mustard don't shift too readily.

'We'll pay for a cleaning job, naturally,' said the cowboy.

I struggled back into the jacket, inspecting myself.

'Just an accident,' I assured him. 'These things happen.'

'Nice of you to take it that way.'

Outside, there was no sign of the man who'd caused the mishap. The bartender extended a ten-dollar bill.

'Customer left,' he explained. 'But he left this to pay for another sandwich, and a drink to go with it. No hard feelings, he hoped.'

'Forget the sandwich,' I told him. 'I'll take a scotch, though. Over ice.'

While he was getting it, I walked over to Ma Kelly's doorstep and looked in. Angela Proctor and her escort were missing. I said a word, and went back quickly to the main entrance, ignoring the voice which called.

'Hey mister, your drink.'

The evening sun was low now, but there was still enough light for me to be certain of one thing.

The white Packard was gone.

CHAPTER THREE

The following morning I walked into the office just before ten o'clock. The city had already begun to go into its steam-bath routine, and the cool of the office was welcome. Even the cool welcome from Florence Digby was welcome.

'My, my,' she greeted. 'Couldn't we sleep?'

La Digby is what you might call the pivot of the organisation, if that's the word I'm looking for. She makes the thing work. I'm not too strong on little matters of administration, like writing letters and reports, keeping a record system, sending out bills. Left to my own devices, I'd probably wind up back on Crane Street, but Florence isn't about to leave me to my devices. In fact she doesn't altogether approve of some of my little ways, and my flexible view of office hours is a case in point.

'Stake-out last night,' I mumbled, by way of a peace-offering. 'Any word from Sam Thompson?'

'He telephoned about twenty minutes ago. Said he'd be here around ten o'clock. Why, goodness me,' she added brightly. 'It's that now.'

'So it is,' I grunted, marching towards the door.

'Oh, Mr. Preston.'

I turned to see her holding out a buff-coloured envelope.

'This was delivered by hand this morning.'

I ripped it open. Inside was a check for twenty-five dollars, made out to me. There was a printed slip from Buck's Rancho, and the words typed on 'To cover cost of cleaning one suit'. There was no signature. I looked at my name again, to be sure there was no mistake, but I knew there wouldn't be. What had been no more than a remote suspicion the night before, was now an obvious fact. The man in the white Packard had spotted the tail. He'd taken me to a place where he had friends who would do little things for him. Such as tipping Round-up Specials over people who took too close an interest in his comings and goings. Nobody had asked my name, nobody went through my pockets. But somebody took time out to investigate my car, and after that it would have been easy. The check was the clincher. We know who you are, we know where to find you. That put them one ahead of me on the board. Unsatisfactory.

I fished in my pocket, and came out with the license number of the white Packard.

'Run a check on that for me, Florence. Let me have the name and address of the owner.'

'Very well.'

I went through then, to the silent calm of my own office. There was a small pile of mail for me to read through. Pushing it to one side, I placed the source of my new wealth in the centre of the desk, and stared at it without love.

'Huh,' I snorted.

I picked up the first letter on the pile. Some financial genius was offering exclusive mineral rights to one quarter acre of the moon's surface for only one hundred and fifty dollars. For five hundred I could have a whole acre to myself. The moon, it seemed, would be the new Texas, and this was my chance to get in on the ground floor. I thought about it, and decided that the gravity problem of the ten-gallon hat would be the downfall of the scheme. I filed the letter in the waste basket and picked up the next one.

The buzzer sounded.

'Sam Thompson is here.'

'Push him through.'

The door opened, and Thompson shambled in. Some people walk. Others charge, flit or tramp. Thompson shambles. A tall, heavy, sleepy-looking character, he always contrives, standing or sitting, to remain shapeless. I've even seen him shapeless when he was stretched unconscious on the ground.

'Morning Sam, have a seat.'

He slumped into a chair, hands plunged deep into the baggy pockets of his crumpled linen jacket.

'How did it go?' I queried.

After the disappointment of losing the Packard the previous evening, I had no ambition to spend who knew how many hours waiting for Angela Proctor to return home to Roseland Drive. So I called up Sam Thompson, a very reliable leg-man when he had his thirst in check, and asked him to keep an eye on things.

'Well now, let's see,' he began ponderously. 'I came on duty at eight o'clock—'

'—eight thirty,' I corrected. Sam is careless about money matters.

'I'm charging my time from when I left the house,' he said indignantly. He didn't have a house. Just two rooms in a fleabag at the wrong end of town. 'Nothing happened until just before midnight. Then this Packard you gave me, that turned up, and drove to the subject's house. Car stayed on the drive maybe three minutes. Nobody got out. I can't imagine what they were doing in there. Then the subject got out, alone, and went into the house. The guy in the Packard backed around, and drove away.'

'Did you follow him?'

'What for? We can find out who he is without much trouble. No, I stayed on a while, in case the subject decided to make another journey. The lights downstairs were all switched on. The upstairs was dark. I began to think it was a bust, but I decided to stay on anyway, until the lady went to bed. At twelve

46

forty-five, we got a break. A little Toyota came down the road, turned into the subject's driveway. A man got out and was admitted to the house at once.'

'Did you get a look at him?'

'Not then. Look, let me tell it how it happened, will you? Like I say, the guy went inside. Aha, thinks I, now we'll see whether the upstairs lights get a play. But no. Whatever happened, happened downstairs. The guy stayed thirty minutes, then left. This time, I decided there wouldn't be any more callers that night. It was already one fifteen in the a.m. I thought I'd follow the Toyota. We went right into town, to the Granville Apartments. That's down on—'

'—I know where it is. Go on.'

'Right. The guy parks the car, gives the night-manager a big hello, and goes up in the elevator. He lives there, right? So I went to this night-manager, and flashed him a Lone Ranger badge or something. The guy is named Brasselle, Gus Brasselle. He's been living in the joint about three months, keeps his nose clean, pays the rent. And what about this Mr. Brasselle? What does he do for a crust, do we imagine?'

'I give up.'

'He's in your racket. A private investigator, that's what he is. Or that's what he says he is. He doesn't have an office, and he isn't listed anywhere that I can trace. But that's what the man says.'

'H'm.'

So, whatever Angela and the Packard driver might be up to, they weren't getting up to it in her house. She didn't even have the guy in for a drink, after having been out with him the whole evening. Then, when he's safely clear, she has an appointment with another man. Again, it would seem to be on the harmless side, if the lighting arrangements meant anything. It would seem more likely that this Brasselle was working for the lady, and had gone to the house to make some kind of a report, at a time when neither of them was likely to be spotted.

But that's the trouble with my imagination. Always leaping ahead to conclusions, without nearly enough by way of hard facts.

'What kind of a looking guy was this Brasselle?'

'Five ten, one eighty, good shape, neat dresser, dark hair, no whiskers.'

'Age?'

'Late twenties, early thirties. Round there.'

'Good. A useful job you did there, Sam. Go home and put your feet up. I'll call you this afternoon, let you know what's going on.'

'Er, my rent is about due—'

'Sam,' I cut in, 'you'll get paid when the job is done. I can't afford to have you out hooraying the town when we have work to do. You think the night-manager will tell Brasselle you were around, asking questions?'

He gave me that slow smile.

'I doubt it. I made a deal with him. He'd forget I'd been there, and I'd forget how many fire regulations he was busting.'

'One more thing. The number of the apartment.'

'One-oh-one.'

The Granville Apartments isn't exactly the Monkton Hilton, but it isn't Slumville either. If this Gus Brasselle had been living there for some months, then whatever he was doing was producing a nice steady income. A private investigator, forsooth. People like us ought to keep in touch more. Maybe I should pay him a social call.

'Thanks Sam, I'll call you later.'

Thompson and Florence Digby crossed in the doorway. He stood back to make room for her, giving the movement plenty of exaggeration. She pretended to sniff as she passed, and I watched this pantomime with a dead pan. There was always some kind of chemistry between these two, and I never had been able to pin it down. The door closed and Florence said,

'That car, the Packard.'

'Oh yes.'

'Registered to a George Tuscano. Here's the address.'

Tuscano. Tuscano. I kept turning the name over in my head.

'There's something familiar about it, I'm certain, but I can't pin it down. George Tuscano. Well, thanks Florence.'

'Aren't you going to ask me?'

I looked at her in surprise.

'Ask you what?'

'Ask me if the name means anything.'

She waited in quiet triumph, forcing me to go through the whole charade.

'All right, Miss Digby, tell me. Does the name George Tuscano mean anything to you?'

'I should hope so. He's one of the Tuscano brothers. There are three of them. This one, George, he's the eldest. He's forty one. Then there's Alberto, thirty seven, and the one they call the baby, Tony. He's only twenty eight. They all came here together, just over a year ago, after a difference of opinion with some other—ah—business man in Las Vegas. We had a bulletin on them at the time, through our press service, for which we pay a large sum every three months. The bulletin is in its proper place on the file. But you don't go in much for files, do you?'

Women never learn the rules about fighting. After the referee has counted the loser out, you don't go on slamming into him.

'Enough, enough.' I held up a hand. 'I wonder, Miss Digby, if I could trouble you for the bulletin on the Tuscano brothers?'

She already had it in her hand, folded. Now, she placed it in front of me, smoothing it flat

50

with relish.

'Thank you,' I acknowledged, coldly.

Originally from San Francisco, the Tuscanos had led a lively existence. George, with the privilege of age, naturally led the way, through auto-theft, break and enter, assault with a deadly weapon, and so on, up the scale. Finally they made it to 'known gambler', which doesn't sound very terrible when you just read the words. In any case, in Las Vegas they were perfectly entitled to the description, which carried no more smear in that great city than ice-cream salesman would in any other. But they weren't top-ranking people, the brothers Tuscano, and when they got a little too ambitious, certain of the vested interests had explained to them that desert air was not good for lungs accustomed to the tang of sea-salt in the breeze. They got the message, and decided to move back to the coast. Only this time, instead of heading home, they thought they'd give us people in the south a break, and here they were.

I wondered what they were doing these days, apart from squiring headstrong beauties around. It probably wasn't anything I'd want my old maiden aunt to know about.

By and large, this Angela Proctor thing was taking some kind of shape quite early. Already I had her tied in with a trio of well-documented hoodlums on the one hand, and a so-called private eye who had no office, on the other. Not bad, for one evening.

But there, my imagination was leaping and twisting around again. I was going to have to stop that.

I riffled through the drawers of the desk until I came up with an official document which described me as a Deputy Sheriff of Wahoo County, or somewhere. I tried to recall the circumstances which brought me the distinction, but could only recall an hilarious all-night poker game with the City Hall crowd. If I'd stopped a runaway horse, they'd have probably made me Town Marshall.

I inserted the paper into my billfold, with all the official stamps showing, and closed the drawer. Then I went outside, where Florence was clacking away on her typewriter.

'Have to go out,' I informed her. 'I'll probably look in again some time in the afternoon.'

She regarded me frostily.

'Is there a number where I could reach you?'

'No. I'll be moving around. Oh, and if a Mr. Shoemaker calls, tell him I'm out looking for a flywheel. He'll know what you mean.'

Her face thawed sufficiently to register disbelief.

'Shoemaker? And you did say flywheel?'

'Right,' I assured her. 'That's detective talk. Kind of a code.'

'Is it all right if I carry on with this report in

52

plain English?'

'I'll see you.'

*   *   *

The Granville Apartments is across town, and sufficiently far from the docks to qualify as respectable. I got stuck at a traffic light when I was almost there. There was a flash of red in the crossing traffic up ahead, and I was just able to identify the car as an M.G., without seeing the driver. I told myself not to get so fancy with the mindwork. It's a popular car, and there were probably fifty like it within a reckonable radius.

I made a left turn in the direction the sport car had come from, and was soon locking my doors outside the address I wanted. Inside, a man looked at me without much interest.

'Are you the manager here?' I clipped, very official.

'That's me,' he confirmed.

'Sheriff's Office. I'm Deputy Preston.'

My voice and my attitude were those of a man who was on business, a man who was already suffering from the heat, and didn't want any nonsense from apartment building managers. He scarcely saw the buzzer, just the black, official stamps.

'What's up, officer?'

'You have a tenant here, Apartment 101, name of Brasselle. Is he home?'

53

He turned to look at the In-Out board on the wall behind him.

'Well,' he hedged, 'according to that thing he's upstairs. But then again, people go in and out when I'm not looking. Do you know, some of them even use the rear entrance. I mean, how am I supposed to do my job, with people carrying on that way?'

His voice had dropped automatically into the whining, defensive tone, held in ready reserve for officials of all varieties.

'Must be rough,' I clucked. 'Never mind, I'll go up and see.'

'I could call him up,' he offered, gesturing towards the small switchboard.

'No,' I said, sharply. 'Leave that thing alone.'

His hands seemed to freeze in mid-gesture as I went to the elevator.

'Third floor,' he called.

I nodded, pushed three, and the doors closed. Upstairs, I found myself in an airless corridor, smelling musty and confined. Nobody answered the bell at one-oh-one. I tried again, then banged on the door. Still no reply. The lock was old-fashioned, and at the second try I felt the tumblers click round. I slipped master keys back into my pocket, and turned the handle.

'Brasselle?'

I pushed the door wider, and went inside, closing it softly behind me.

It was a two-roomed apartment, and the tenant was in the other one. He lay on his face beside the bed, fingers crooked as they had tried to dig into the carpet, away from the agony of the heavy slugs someone had pumped into his back. There were three of the ragged bloody holes in the yellow pyjama top. He was naked from the waist down. The description I'd had from Sam Thompson had been close enough for me to decide the man on the floor was Brasselle. His skin was cold to the touch, but I'm no medical man. All I knew was he'd been alive until close to two o'clock that morning. Now he was dead, and anything he might have been able to tell me was gone forever.

I got up from the floor, and began to poke around. There wasn't very much of interest. He seemed to lead a quiet, bachelor kind of existence, tidier than most. A leather wallet had been tossed carelessly onto a bedside table. It told me nothing, except that Brasselle had owned one five dollar bill and four singles. No driving license, no identifying documents of any kind. I ran my fingers carefully around each of the small compartments. Nothing. Then I had an idea, and took out the currency bills. In one corner of the now-empty slot was a small, crumpled piece of paper. I scraped it out, and opened it. It said, in a hasty pencil scrawl:

'Iris Moorland
2425 New Monastery Drive'

The name meant nothing to me. I put the scrap of paper in an inside pocket and replaced the money. I could tell by the way his property was stacked, that someone had been ahead of me in searching the dead man's stuff. Whether they hoped to find something, or whether the object was to remove any item which could identify Brasselle, I had no way of knowing. Certainly there was nothing which could give a lead as to who the corpse might be, or where he came from. There was one thing which had been overlooked, a small brown leather shoulder strap with a neat pouch. It might not have meant much to most people, but to me it spelled 'gun', and that made Mr. Brasselle a man who carried a concealed weapon.

I stood in the center of the outer room, staring around and wondering whether something obvious was staring me in the face. If it was, I couldn't see it, and there wasn't to be any time for second-guessing. Outside was the unmistakeable wail of the police siren, and it was drawing closer by the second. Maybe it was headed in my direction, and maybe not, but I don't take chances on things like that.

I left the apartment, rubbing at any surface where I could have left a print, and pulled the door shut. As I straightened up, a man came walking along the corridor. He looked at me curiously, so I banged on the door I'd just closed.

'Brasselle,' I shouted. 'C'mon open up.'

Then I banged again. The man made no bones about his interest now.

'Quick,' I snapped. 'Is there a rear way out of here? He hasn't come out through the front door.'

'Why yes. Through that door at the end there.'

'Thank you.'

I made off quickly, and the man rushed away to tell his wife all about the excitement. I was sitting in my car across the street when the blue and orange prowler screeched to a halt outside the main entrance.

CHAPTER FOUR

I needed a chance to think, and a cool place to do it. Years before, someone had realised the need for such a place, and opened it up under the name of Sam's Bar. There were a number of other thinkers of view when I got there, and I knew several of them well enough to nod.

'Getting hot outside, Sam,' I greeted.

'That's why the beer is cold,' he replied mechanically, beginning to fill a mug.

He'd probably had the same high-toned

57

conversation fifty times before that day, with every expectation of fifty more ahead of him. I spread a five on the counter.

'Let me have some change for the phone, will you?'

While he was counting out, I sipped at the frosted mug. The beer was just like always, the best in town. There was a table close by the small row of phone-booths, and I went to park, keeping an eye on the time. Mr. Shoemaker had been very explicit about the times he could be contacted. One of the periods was eleven forty five to twelve noon. It was now just after eleven thirty, and I sat thinking about the wording of the conversation to come. It was important to get across certain points to my client, and at the same time to bear in mind the strong possibility of a wire-tap. With someone as prominent as the man I would be talking to, it would be a matter of routine for certain people to keep their ears open. What I had to say would make profitable listening for his enemies.

At eleven forty five exactly, I dialled the number. The receiver at the other end was lifted immediately.

'Mr. Shoemaker?' I queried.

There was no mistaking his voice when he replied.

'I think you must have the wrong number. Who is that speaking please?'

'The name is Flywheel,' I told him.

58

'Hold the phone away from your ear,' he commanded.

I didn't understand him, but I did it anyway, and none too soon. A high-pitched whine blasted out from the ear-piece. If I'd held it closer, the noise would have bored a hole clean through my skull. It faded mercifully away.

'Mr. Flywheel, are you still there?'

Gingerly, I brought the phone back where it should be. No ill effects.

'Yes, I'm still here, but the phone almost melted.'

He chuckled.

'Sorry about that, Flywheel. New gadget. Ruinous to bugging devices. It takes minutes to get the things back in action. You may speak quite freely.'

Well, well. Every day something new.

'I've been keeping an eye on that person you and I were talking about,' I began.

'Really? And has anything interesting come to light?'

'Yes, it has. Around one o'clock this morning, a man called at the house. I had someone watching the place.'

He cut in, before I had a chance to finish.

'I'm disappointed, Flywheel. I wasn't expecting this kind of stuff. She's entitled to her private life, you know.'

'Wait a minute,' I insisted. 'I wouldn't call just to tell you that. The point is, I found out who the man was. Matter of routine. It turned out he was someone in my line of work. At least, that's what he claimed to be. I thought I'd go and have a talk with him this morning. When I got close to where he lives, I saw someone I think may have been your daughter driving away.'

'What of it?'

I wished he wouldn't keep interrupting that way.

'I called on this man. Somebody else got there first. Whoever this somebody was, they killed him.'

I waited for the reaction. There was silence for a while.

'Are you saying that my daughter—?'

'I'm not putting any construction on it at all. I'm simply telling you the facts. The man is dead. Murdered. The place is an apartment house, and the manager knows I was there. It shouldn't take police too long to get on my tail. That doesn't worry me too much. We've had many a little talk over the years. But if this manager also saw your daughter, we could have a whole new game.'

'Yes.' He paused, thinking. 'But you weren't absolutely certain it was she? You said so.'

'She'. Not 'her'. Nice.

'No, I'm not. But what I think isn't relevant, because I'm not about to pass anything like that over to the homicide people. A little matter like withholding information concerning a capital offense won't keep me from sleeping. The point is, I won't have any control over what the manager has to say.'

'Ah. Quite. Tell me about him. Do you think you might be able to persuade him to suffer a little loss of memory?'

Back to the good green folding dollar. I sighed.

'What I may have been able to do is no longer in point, Mr. Shoemaker. I just managed to beat it out of the back door, as the law was coming in at the front. Whatever the guy has to tell will have been told by now.'

'Damn,' he breathed. 'So what are you suggesting ought to be done?'

'There's nothing useful I can come up with,' I said regretfully. 'I can stall the boys in blue. I've done it before, and they won't get too mad at me. Not at this early stage, anyway. But that won't help the lady, if they get wise to her involvement. As I said before, all I'm doing is reporting what I know.'

'And I appreciate it,' he assured me heavily. 'Appreciate it very much indeed. You seem to have a knack of being around when things happen. What will you do now? Lie low for a while?'

'Lord no, I didn't kill anybody, so there's nothing for me to worry about. I'll just get on with what you hired me to do. With this new development, that could become more urgent than ever, and for different reasons.'

'Different reasons?'

He sounded mystified.

'Certainly. We're now in a murder situation. If that has any connection with whatever your daughter is doing, then there could be danger for her, too. I'm not saying that is likely, but we can't rule it out as impossible. Oh, I'll have plenty to keep me busy.'

'Yes, I see that. Thank you. You'll keep me posted?'

'Whenever there's anything to report,' I assured him. 'And if there's no phone call for twenty four hours or so, don't worry about it. It'll probably be because the police toss me in the can for the night. They do that sometimes if they're mad enough. It won't be serious.'

He chuckled tightly.

'I must say—er—Flywheel, you seem to be the right man for this particular job.'

'Let's hope I come up with the right answers, Mr. Shoemaker.'

We said goodbye, and I hung up. When I got back to the table, my beer was flat.

*   *   *

When I got back to the office, Florence Digby was getting ready to leave for her lunch break.

'Any calls?' I asked her.

'No,' she replied. 'I was about to break off, but if you need anything—?'

The police evidently hadn't got around to

me yet.

'Nothing thanks. But lock the outer door will you? Leave the "Gone to Lunch" on display. That way I won't be disturbed.'

'Very well.'

I went and sat behind my fancy desk to think. A minute later, I heard the click of the lock from outside, and I was safe from intrusions for thirty minutes or so. The directory gave me the office number of the Ad-Hoc people, and I dialled and waited.

'This is the Ad-Hoc organisation. Good afternoon.'

The voice was bright and friendly, and I could picture the girl as one of those young, earnest characters, with the big black hornrims and the scraped-back hair.

'I'd like to speak with Mrs. Proctor, please.'

'I don't believe she's in the building at present. If you hang on I will check.'

It took her two minutes to ask around. Very thorough.

'Are you still there? Sorry to keep you. Mrs. Proctor called in sick today. Can someone else help you?'

'Er no. No thanks.'

I hung up, and considered this new information. It had been my intention to stay clear of Angela Proctor, if it were possible. But if she hadn't reported for work, that meant she was out loose somewhere, and I didn't care for the thought. Whatever connection she had

63

with Brasselle had brought them together in the small hours. Shortly after that, somebody killed the man. That seemed to leave two possibilities. In the first place, the girl could herself be in danger. In the second place, she might have killed the man personally. The third alternative, that there was no tie-up, and that Brasselle had been bumped off for entirely other reasons, I dismissed as too remote.

If she was in trouble, of whatever kind, I had better get involved before it got worse. It was a pity that I had to show my hand, but there seemed to be no way to avoid it. The telephone number was among the stuff her father had given me, I pushed buttons with reluctant fingers.

Her voice was guarded.

'Hallo?'

'Mrs. Proctor?'

'Who is this?'

'We haven't met, Mrs. Proctor, but there are things going on that we ought to talk about.'

'I don't understand. Who are you? What things?'

I hedged.

'I don't trust telephones. I could be out at the house in twenty minutes. You really ought to talk to me. Maybe if I was to tell you I was at the Granville Apartments this morning, it'll give you some idea what this is all about. I'm doing you a favor, Mrs. Proctor. What I ought to be doing is talking to the police.'

I could hear the sharp intake of breath.

'I fail to see why it should interest me what you do,' she said imperiously. 'But I suppose there's no harm in talking to you. You seem to know where I live?'

'I'll be there in twenty minutes,' I confirmed.

Then I broke the connection, before she had time to change her mind. I pushed out Sam Thompson's number, and waited for the familiar sleepy growl. We talked for a couple of minutes, and then it was time for me to leave. At the door of the office I paused, changed my mind, and went back to the desk. From it, I removed a blue-black Smith and Wesson thirty eight caliber Police Special, and looked at it thoughtfully. By and large, I'm not in favour of guns. They have a tendency to go off and hurt people, which is something they can't do while they're tucked safely away in desk-drawers. But there was somebody out there who felt differently about them. Differently enough to bump off Gus Brasselle. If I came up against this character, it would be no occasion for a philosophical chat about desk-drawers. I wiped surplus oil from the outside of the weapon and stuck it in my waistband.

As I let myself out, the phone was ringing.

The early afternoon heat was slowing everybody down as I headed away from the

65

city, and I made good time out to Roseland Drive. I drove past the Proctor place slowly. There was the familiar red M.G., parked close up to the house. It was the only car on view. I reversed at the end of the street, and came back, parking outside. Then I walked up the incline, which had been made easier by inserting huge stone flags into the earth every few feet. It was a pleasant front aspect, with ornamental colored bushes stuck here and there in the kind of casual way that denotes a lot of care and attention. I wondered about that. Angela Proctor didn't have the kind of reputation that went with outdoor work of that kind.

The front door was an ornate Spanish-style affair in white-painted wood. It stood open, revealing a dark, cool-looking interior. I rang at the ball, and waited. No one answered, so I tried again, with the same result.

'Mrs. Proctor?' I called inside.

I began to feel uneasy. She had to be somewhere around, surely? The car was outside, the door was wide open. I tried calling out her name once more. Nobody answered. I took a tentative step inside and looked around, adjusting my eyes to the gloom. Then I had a better idea, and went back out into the sun, skirting the outside of the house, and looking in at the windows. There was nothing on view but furniture. I made it all the way round to the rear, still seeing no one. Then I saw the

66

pool, a pear-shaped gleam of cool blue water with pieces of colored furniture dotted around. At the far end, reclining on a rest-easy, was the woman I'd come to see.

Angela Proctor was as good as her photographs, only better. A tall, strongly built girl, of beautiful proportions, with skin of a light golden tan gleaming faintly in the sunlight. We were giving the skin plenty of air today, with only two thin strips of yellow material to disqualify the wearer from the Nudist of the Year title. One of the strips was up around here, and the other was down there, and they didn't leave much to the imagination. Especially the one up around here. She was facing towards me, and the enormous dark glasses prevented anyone from being able to tell whether she was awake or asleep.

'Mrs. Proctor?' I asked, unnecessarily.

She summoned enough energy to twitch one hand in a beckoning gesture. I walked forward. When I was about ten feet away, she said,

'Please sit down. There.'

'There' was a wood-framed canvas seat. I parked in it, inspecting her.

'What's your name?'

Coming from where it did, the voice ought to have been one of those warm, lazy sounds. Instead, it was crisp and businesslike.

'Preston. Mark Preston.'

'Really? It's rather pleasant. I would have expected something like Chuck. Yes, that would be better. Chuck Snyder, I think. I shall call you Snyder. It's more in keeping with what you are. Tell me Snyder, can you read?'

I grinned, and sat back.

'I agree with you about names. They don't always suit people, do they? Take you, for instance. Lying around like an ad. for a girlie magazine. There's no Angela about you at all. Irma would be better. Say, Irma La Verne. I'll bet your hobbies are studying Rembrandt, and listening to early Chinese water music. In between shows, that is. Sure, Irma, I can read.'

She slid the glasses a fraction down the splendid nose, and a small frown of puzzlement appeared on her forehead.

'You are the man who telephoned, I take it?'

'Sure. I got your number from the Friendly Escort Bureau. I've brought the money with me. In cash, like they said.'

That brought quick red into the smooth cheeks.

'Who the hell do you think you're talking to?'

'Nobody special,' I shrugged. 'Just a typical over-priced Irma. A rich-bitch who's had everything of her own way for so many years, she thinks it's the natural order of things. I've been high-hatted by experts, lady. You've a lot to learn.'

There was a huge striped towel beside her. Sliding a hand underneath it, she came up with an ugly flat automatic, and pointed it in the wrong direction. At me, that is.

'I was wondering how you would look with an extra hole in your face,' she said casually.

I didn't understand this new development. I didn't like it either, because I could tell from the casual grip of her fingers that she'd held one of those things before.

'Murder?' I queried. 'That's pretty rugged, even from you. And would you mind telling me why?'

My intention had been to maintain the bantering tone of the conversation, but my voice-box didn't seem to be cooperating too well.

'Murder?' she echoed. 'No, I don't think so. You're a prowler. This is private property. I'm a wealthy woman, and all unprotected in the world. With the kind of law I can hire, I'll probably get a commendation.'

'You still didn't tell me why,' I reminded.

Her face was taut.

'Because you and your kind make me sick. Outside of child-molesting, I rank the blackmailer at the bottom of the heap.'

I sighed with inward relief.

'Blackmail? Is that why you think I'm here? Well, you can put that thing away, lady. You have me all wrong.'

She was right. From that angle it would make a hole in my face. The muzzle didn't waver.

'You keep on talking,' she invited. 'Convince me.'

'About the gun—'

'The gun stays where it is. Well?'

'The name is Preston, like I said. I'm a private investigator. There's identification in my pocket.'

'Leave it there. Go on.'

'I've been carrying out some work for a client, and—'

'What client?' she snapped.

'Tut tut,' I reproved. 'In my business, the client's identity is confidential. Anyway, while I was doing this work, I came up against a man who claimed to be in my line of work. Name of Gus Brasselle.'

The gun twitched. So did the hair at the back of my scalp.

'You say he claimed to be?' she challenged.

'That's right. I checked him out with the State License Bureau. They have no record on him.'

She bit at her lower lip, with white strong teeth.

'Unlike you.'

'Unlike me,' I admitted. 'They probably have a file two inches thick on me. Not all of it's true.'

'Leave that for a minute. What about this Gus whatever you said?'

Some of the decision was gone from her voice, the tightness. The thing was on the

70

point of turning into a conversation.

'Gus Brasselle was what I said,' I reminded her. 'I thought I ought to have a little chat with old Gus, so I slipped over to the Granville Apartments this morning. Somebody got there first. They also had a little chat with the guy, only they didn't like his end of it. He was somewhat dead when I arrived.'

'Why are you telling me all of this?'

'Because I found a little book with your name and address in it, Mrs. Proctor. And I saw your car driving away, just before I arrived.'

Now that we seemed to have left the blackmail behind, she was looking more and more puzzled. As if on a sudden impulse, she planked the gun down on the towel. It could still be reached, but I was highly relieved to see it pointing elsewhere.

'That doesn't follow,' she objected. 'You say you saw me drive away first, then found my name afterwards. What made you connect the two things?'

There was nothing wrong with her think-box, at least. Hurriedly I improvised.

'Oh, I didn't. Not at that moment. I noticed the car, because that's the way I am. It wasn't until I saw it parked outside your house just now that I put the two things together.'

She took off the heavy glasses, and bit absently at the frame.

'So why are you here? Why didn't you just

71

hand the little book over to the police? You did tell the police, I imagine?'

I shrugged.

'Why would I? Somebody else'll find the body quick enough. I don't have any useful information. You see, if I get mixed up in that kind of stuff, the law boys get very inquisitive. They don't just leave it at the murder, they go on probing into all kinds of things. Like what am I working on, who am I working for, little things like that. No, if I can help them, I do. But there's no point in looking for trouble. I don't know anything about the Brasselle killing.'

I left it dangling around, and she picked it up.

'But you think I might?'

'He thinks you might what?'

We both looked round towards the new voice.

CHAPTER FIVE

The man who had arrived quietly from the direction of the house was dark-haired, stockily built, and at that moment mean-looking. He had a faint resemblance to the man I'd seen behind the wheel of the white Packard the previous evening. Angela said hurriedly,

72

'Nothing, Al. Nothing at all, really. He was just leaving. Weren't you?'

I was puzzled to see a look almost of pleading on her face. What was she afraid of? Him? Me? I didn't get it. Well, it didn't matter to me. Now that we knew who we were, we could always talk again.

'Yes, that's right,' I nodded. 'I have to be getting along.'

I began to walk away. The newcomer stopped in front of me, weight carried forward onto the balls of his feet. I've seen trouble before, and he was trouble.

'Not so fast,' he objected. I'll tell you when to leave, cowboy.'

Al. I wondered whether he could be Alberto Tuscano. The name certainly fitted his appearance, and the reputation would match up with his present street-fighter attitude. I spoke to him like a man who isn't looking for any trouble.

'It's a hot day, Al. Let's not be getting all excited.'

The words and the tone gave him just that little bit of overconfidence I'd been aiming for. Certain that he was dealing with a chump, he relaxed and shoved a hand towards my chest.

'I'll decide—' he began.

He began, but he didn't finish. I dropped my right shoulder, grabbed at the advancing arm and ducked under it. With my right foot I kicked hard at his shin, and swung myself round violently. It was just the way they show you in the text books. Al went sailing in an arc over my shoulder. If I'd misjudged the swing, he would have crashed onto the concrete surround of the pool. But it was my day for getting it right. He missed the edge by a yard and landed like an enraged buffalo in four feet of water. Angela froze where she was. The whole thing had happened so fast, she hadn't quite grasped it all.

The spluttering Al gave a great roar of rage, and began to flounder to the handrail at the side. I knelt down and waited for him to get close. Then I produced the thirty-eight and held it against his forehead, dead center. Beneath the blue shave, he went white.

'You see Al,' I explained gently. 'you must never call a native Californian a cowboy. It hurts our pride.'

His eyes called me many things, cowboy not being included. But there wasn't a thing he could do. A man can hardly adopt a more defenseless attitude than standing in four feet of water with an automatic pistol pressed against his head.

'Who are you?' he breathed.

'You first,' I encouraged. 'After all, it's my party.'

'This time,' he muttered. 'This time.'

'You didn't answer me,' I reproved. 'Maybe you'd like me to hold your head under water for a minute or two?'

He sighed.

'Tuscano,' he shrugged. 'I'm Al Tuscano. You'd better remember it, because you'll be hearing it again.'

'Good. I like people to keep in touch.' I glanced over towards Angela. She had swung her legs down, and was sitting watching the little tableau. The gun beside her was forgotten in the excitement. Somehow I didn't think she was entirely on Al's team. Not for this particular match. I decided to try something. 'Well, I'll be getting along. Don't stay too long in the water, Al. I didn't get around to telling the lady who I was, so I don't think I'll tell you, either. I like to sleep nights.'

The movement of Angela's hand was almost imperceptible, but to me it was a nod. She'd kept quiet about my identity. She was one mysterious lady.

I put the gun out of sight, and walked quickly away. The last thing I saw was Al Tuscano shaking off the helping hand she extended, as he hauled himself out of the pool. In the front of the house, there was now a white Chev parked behind the M.G. Mr. Tuscano had arrived only minutes after me. He was either a casual visitor with an unfortunate sense of timing, or else Angela had sent for him as soon as I telephoned, in which case his timing was very good.

The drive back into town was uneventful, and I kept on gnawing away at my highly unproductive first encounter with Angela Proctor. It hadn't gone at all the way I'd intended, and the climax had only made me an enemy I didn't need. So what had I learned? It had been her car I'd seen leaving the Granville Apartments. Therefore, either she had seen the body and run away, or she had killed Gus Brasselle herself. She had some connection with Al Tuscano, and it was strong enough for him to feel free to wander through the house, without waiting to be invited in. She was willing to keep my identity from him, unless I'd misjudged her expression. Why would she do that? Because to give me away would involve revealing the purpose of my visit. Either she didn't want him to connect me with Brasselle, or, more likely, she didn't want any connection established between the dead man and herself. After all, the late so-called private investigator had reported to her house the previous night, after the elder Tuscano had left. If I was right about the last assumption, she would be having a helluva time explaining my visit to the dripping Alberto. Well, that was her problem, I decided. She hadn't struck me as a lady without resources.

At the office, Florence said,

'Do we know a Mr. Hubbard?'

'Hubbard?'

I fed the name into the program, and a blank sheet came out.

'No Hubbard,' I confessed.

She shrugged.

'Perhaps it was a long time ago. He said he knew you in your Deputy Sheriff days.'

The air seemed unusually still.

'What did he want?'

'He wouldn't say. I have a number here where he can be reached until four o'clock.'

I took the piece of paper from her, and stared at the message.

'Thanks. I'll call him in a few minutes. Was there anything else?'

'Nothing. Were you expecting anyone in particular?'

Florence Digby is a great girl, and I've had good reason to trust her a thousand times. All the same, I make a point of not burdening her with information she doesn't need to have. She certainly had no need to be told that I expected the police to be looking for me. Even less reason to know that there was a small matter of a murder I'd omitted to report. So I said,

'No. No one in particular.'

In my office I took a great gulp of iced water from the cooler, and fresh sweat broke out all over my face, on top of the layer that was already in place. Then I spread out my piece of paper, and began pushing buttons on the telephone.

The receiver at the other end was lifted quickly.

'Hallo?'

'Am I talking to Mr. Hubbard?'

'Speaking,' he confirmed. 'Who is this, please?'

His voice had a will o' the wisp quality, now you hear it, now you don't. Like silk being drawn lightly over a leather cushion. It was faintly familiar, but I couldn't place it.

'I had a message left at my office to call you, Mr. Hubbard. The name is Preston.'

'Ah. I wonder whether you might be the Mr. Preston I'm trying to contact,' he slithered. 'The one I talked with just a few hours ago. We had a most interesting little chat. My Mr. Preston showed me a Deputy Sheriff's identity that he carries. Do you have one of those, Mr. Preston?'

I didn't like the sound of him.

'I might have,' I admitted. 'Tell me more about this conversation you had.'

'Well, it really wasn't a very long talk, you understand,' he replied smoothly. 'Not more than a few words, really. My Mr. Preston had to go upstairs to a party. Soon after that, a lot of his friends arrived. They went up to the party, too. But they missed him. I think he left the party early.'

The only party I'd been to that morning had been the one-man corpse exhibition in the Brasselle apartment.

'His friends must have been disappointed to miss him.'

He laughed gently.

'Well now, you know, I have a little confession to make, Mr. Preston. What with all the excitement and everything, I believe I forgot to mention that he'd been there at all. Very remiss of me, I admit. Now I'm feeling guilty. Maybe Mr. Preston will be mad at me for not telling them. I really don't know what to do. What do you suggest, Mr. Preston? That is, if you're the right man to advise me.'

I had him now. The manager of the Granville Apartments. I'd have got there quicker but for the heat.

'Are you a musical man, Mr. Hubbard?'

'Oh yes, very. Why do you ask?'

'I thought I could hear a theme from the Cash Register Symphony in the background.'

He thought about it.

'There are so few pleasures in life, a man has to take what he can,' he replied. 'I'd like to have a chat about music. How soon could we meet?'

Very soon, I decided. The little creep had kept my name out of Brasselle's murder so far. He didn't do that because he liked my nice kind face. I had better find out what made him tick. And fast, before he changed his mind.

'I could come there now,' I suggested.

He sounded horrified.

'Oh no. That wouldn't do at all, really. The place is much too untidy for visitors. No, I think somewhere outside would be best. How about the Veterans' Memorial? In fifteen minutes.'

'I'll be there.'

I put down the phone, and wiped sweat off my face. Mr. Hubbard had called it pretty close. I would have to get the lead out if I was to reach that cool green square in a quarter of an hour.

The traffic was in a sleepy good humor, and I got to the place with two minutes to spare. There were a few people around, walking slowly, or sitting on the white stone benches which are dotted around. I went and parked on one, close to the veined marble plinth, and lit a cigaret. A few feet along, a crumpled little woman sat weeping silently. Beside her was a bunch of flowers. She'd sit there awhile, and remember, and cry. Then she would get up, search around for a certain name among the hundreds which were chipped into the base of the memorial, and put the flowers down close by. She'd probably stand there a few moments, then wander away to resume whatever it was she was now doing alone. Now that he wasn't there to help her with it. I'd watched the scene before, many times, and it didn't do anything to raise my spirits.

I looked away from her, and concentrated on an unleashed dog which was sniffling around among some rose bushes.

'Excuse me, it is Mr. Preston, isn't it?'

The last time I'd seen that enquiring face, the owner had been all a-twitter in the entrance of the Granville Apartments.

'Right. Sit down, Mr. Hubbard.'

He sat beside me. The crumpled woman moved away, and we had the bench to ourselves. Now that we were alone, there was no need for the pussyfoot dialogue we'd been using on the telephone.

'Go ahead, Hubbard. It's your party. Start by telling me why you didn't give my name to the cops.'

My directness seemed to catch him unawares. He'd been preparing for a more delicate kind of exchange.

'You're very blunt,' he complained.

'My psychiatrist is working on it,' I assured him. 'Well?'

'Well, at first it didn't seem necessary. I mean, you'd shown me your identification. When the others arrived, I thought right away it was all part of the same visit. You had simply got there before the others.'

That made sense.

'And afterwards?'

'They came rushing down again, to say that poor Gus had been murdered. They wanted to know what time I started duty, had I heard anything at all, who had been in and out of the building. It was obvious from some of the questions that Gus had been dead for hours.'

That was the second time he'd called him Gus.

'So?'

'So, I knew it couldn't have been you that killed him, you see?' he explained. 'You had only gone up to the apartment five minutes before.'

'That doesn't explain why you kept my name out of it.'

'No.'

He sat silent for a moment, getting his thoughts in order.

'Gus Brasselle was my cousin,' he said suddenly.

I looked at him then.

'Well, well,' I commented. 'I wondered how he could meet the rental.'

He dropped his eyes.

'He didn't. Not altogether. He was paying about half the correct amount. He came to me a few months ago with a proposition. He had some big case he was working on—'

'—case?'

'—yes. Gus was a private investigator, you know.'

'No, I don't know. Everybody keeps saying that, but I've checked him out. He doesn't have a State license.'

Hubbard nodded.

'I see. Well, I think you may have checked with the wrong state, Mr. Preston. Gus is from Texas.'

'From—? Well, well. He was a long way from home.'

'That appears to have been part of the

plan,' explained Hubbard. 'As a stranger, he would be able to move around more freely than someone local. He wouldn't attract attention.'

He waited for my reaction. I threw away my cigaret. It landed too close to the dog, who glared at me balefully, and trotted away in disdain.

'That makes sense,' I told him. 'Tell me about this big case.'

Hubbard smiled deprecatingly.

'Oh, I don't believe I'm going to do that. Not right away, We don't know each other, Mr. Preston. All I know about you is that you have a Deputy Sheriff's badge—'

'—and a State license—'

'—and a State license,' he agreed. 'You also have an interest in Gus. Did have, at least. I think we're in a barter situation, you and I. I've already shown my good faith, by holding back your name from the authorities. It would seem fair if you made some little concession on your side.'

'You mean, like money?'

He shrugged.

'What else is there? You can't imagine what it's like, to be born with a name like mine. That empty cupboard in the old rhyme, it haunts you all your life. A man likes to keep a few bones, in case he ever buys a dog.'

I looked at his clothes, his shoes. Thought about his job, and his probable credit rating.

'You're one ahead, Mr. Hubbard, keeping me out of it the way you did. I imagine a man could buy a lot of bones for a hundred bucks.'

He drew away from me in horror.

'A hundred? One hundred dollars?' he repeated incredulously. 'Oh no, Mr. Preston. I don't think you have the measure of this situation at all. I'm talking about important matters here, and you're offering me cab-fare.'

He meant it. He wasn't just hanging on for an extra twenty. I began to think Mr. Hubbard might prove to be a real find. But I gave him an impassive stare, keeping my new interest off my face.

'I don't follow you,' I admitted. 'What kind of money did you have in mind?'

He glanced around, to be certain there was no one within earshot. Then he let me have both barrels.

'The smallest amount, the very smallest amount I could consider, would be ten thousand.'

Wow. I expelled breath in a low, whooshing sound.

'That's a whole lot of money. I don't have any authority to talk in terms that big. What would it buy?'

'Information,' he replied primly. 'Information that would lead to other things. Big things. Big people. Where even ten thousand dollars would begin to sound like cab-fare. Obviously, I'm wasting my time. This thing is over your head. Fortunately, I have another market.'

'Who would that be?'

Sometimes a direct and crazy question catches people off balance, and they give you the answer. Not this time. Hubbard smiled sadly.

'Really, Mr. Preston. You must think I'm a complete fool.'

'No. You're wrong there. I don't think anything of the kind. Look, as I say, I can't just make an offer that size. Not by myself. But I can refer to somebody. Somebody who can meet that ten times over. When can we talk again?'

It would be hours yet before I could make contact with Mr. Shoemaker. The need was to keep Hubbard on the boil. He was looking disappointed.

'Time is not on my side,' he demurred. 'The kind of merchandise I'm offering is very dangerous stuff. It could go off and kill somebody. Gus is proof of that. What I want is to cash up and move on. Quickly.'

'Ten o'clock,' I said quickly. 'Give me till ten o'clock. I'll be able to tell you whether we have a deal.'

He hesitated.

'But no later,' he insisted. 'This is my chance to make a score, Mr. Preston. Maybe the only chance I'll ever have. I don't want to do it wrong.'

85

'You'll be at the Apartments?'

'From six,' he confirmed.

'Then I'll be in touch. Don't worry, I'm too interested to fool around.'

He got to his feet.

'Very well. I'll be waiting for your call.'

He went away then, his spare, upright figure lost quickly among people and trees.

I made my thoughtful way back to the car.

CHAPTER SIX

There was nothing to pull me into the office, so I went home to Parkside. My apartment block is very much on the right side of the tracks. I don't have anybody to provide for, and there's no point in saving for my old age. The private cop dodge is an uncertain business, and not very many of us get to an age where we're concerned about the number of gadgets on the wheelchair. Gus Brasselle was the latest statistic in that department.

I broke out some frosted beer, and paddled around the place, shedding clothes, and thinking about the Tuscano brothers. I must be getting to be quite an item on their calendar. Already I'd been warned off by the eldest brother, George. Since then I'd helped Alberto with his swimming lessons. Angela Proctor may have held back on my name, but when the two men compared notes, it wouldn't take long to come up Preston. There was only one brother I hadn't seen so far, and that was Tony. He was just as tough a customer as the others, if the reports were to be believed, and I was in no hurry to make his acquaintance. The family sounded like bad news for a girl like Angela, but maybe that's just the snob in me. After all, a girl who already had one second-rate bullfighter, and a Marseilles dock-rat on her score card, could scarcely raise her skirts in horror when the home-grown variety happened along. At least, this time, she had the nationality right.

The phone blatted away, and Sam Thompson enquired tiredly whether I would be staying home for a while.

'An hour or so, anyway,' I told him. 'What gives?'

'Not much. I'll come over and tell you about it.'

'Right.'

I took a shower, and put on some fresh linen. I was still barefoot when the door-buzzer sounded. Sam must have hurried, I reflected. He probably had a mental image of the cold beer he was certain to get. I slid back the bolt on the door, and began to open it.

Immediately the door was slammed violently open, knocking me backwards into the room. I tripped from the force of the blow, and sat down, shaking my head.

Three men stood inside, grinning down at me.

'Surprise, surprise,' said George Tuscano.

The grin on Al's face was very thin, I noted. The young one, Tony, seemed genuinely amused. None of them was waving any hardware. But, at three to one, who needs it? Particularly when the one isn't even wearing shoes. I backed away along the floor, scrambling to my feet.

'Ain't very polite, is he?' queried Al.

George nodded.

'That's right enough, Preston. You didn't even ask us in.'

'You're already in,' I snapped.

When Tony spoke, his voice didn't grate like the others. Maybe he finished the third grade after all.

'Say, that beer looks good. Ask us to have some, why don't you?'

In case I turned him down, he went off to look for it.

'What do you guys want?'

I hoped my voice sounded more off-hand than I was feeling.

'Just a little chat,' explained George, marching inside. 'Kind of a good neighbor visit, you know? Get acquainted.'

'I already got acquainted,' snarled Al. 'He ain't no good neighbor of mine.'

'Now, now,' reproved George. 'We've been through all that. You're forgetting your manners, Al. It ain't polite to dust a guy over in his own joint.'

Al was itching to come at me, and I didn't take my eyes off his face for a second.

'Look what I got,' announced Tony.

He came back towards us, clutching beer cans.

'That's nice of you, Preston,' nodded George. 'Why don't we sit down, and drink our beer. You sit there. The host oughta sit where all the visitors can see him. Ain't that right, Tony?'

'That's right, big brother.'

If I was going to get a workout, it wasn't going to happen right away, evidently. I sat where George pointed, and he grunted his approval.

'Here.'

Tony tossed one of the cans towards me. I caught it, and set it down beside me.

'See that? Regular little shortstop ain't he?' George exclaimed admiringly.

'He catches cans,' snorted Al. 'People he throws.'

George nodded thoughtfully.

'That's right,' he agreed. 'Why do you do that, Preston? Toss people through the air that way? It can be kind of upsetting.'

'It kind of upset me,' growled Al.

I spread my hands, frowning.

'Al was coming at me,' I replied evenly. 'He's a well-built man, brother Al. Pretty good shape, I would say. Not a guy to fold after one punch. I thought I had a choice to make. I could stand around in the hot sun, having a brawl, or I could stop it fast. I stopped it. The way I did that, nobody got hurt.'

George sucked thirstily at his frosted can. It sounded like feeding time in the dog kennels. Tony chuckled.

'Fast with the hands, fast with the words,' complained George, wiping surplus froth from his chin. 'The way you tell it, everybody ought to toss everybody else in pools.'

'It's better than a busted skull,' I insisted.

Al began to get up.

'Yeah? Who would have got their skull busted, do you suppose?'

It was Tony who put a restraining hand on his shoulder.

'Hold on there, old brother. We can have a nice time breaking him up later. First we have to keep him in a fit state to talk. Am I right, George?'

'Right.' George explained to me. 'Tony's the smart one, you see. Big education, all that stuff. Yes, he's got a head on him, that Tony.'

'If he likes it where it is, you'd better keep him away from me,' I told him.

'Now, now, there you go again. Why are you annoying the lady, Preston? Mrs. Proctor. Why are you doing that?'

'Who says I'm annoying her?' I hedged.

Al rooted around in his pockets, came out

90

with a cheroot and lit it. Short angry puffs of smoke drifted upwards.

I thought quickly. Angela Proctor may have told those birds about our conversation, and then again she may not. As best I could recall, I hadn't said enough to reveal my hand, because there hadn't been time. Al had interrupted too soon. They all waited.

'A man was killed this morning,' I continued. 'He was murdered, as a matter of fact. I wanted to talk to that man, but somebody killed him first.'

The three men exchanged quick glances.

'What's that got to do with—' began Al, but George shook his head at him.

'Keep talking, Preston,' he invited.

'There was a tie-in between the dead man and Mrs. Proctor. I went to talk to her about it.'

I stopped, and reached for my Old Favorites. The smoke from that cheroot was tickling my nose. Tony snapped his fingers.

'Well, get on with it,' he crackled.

I shrugged.

'That's all. I hadn't been there more than two minutes. Brother Al came busting in like the seventh cavalry. I went home.'

'What did she say about—' began Al.

'Leave it Al.' There was no mistaking the command in George's tone. 'This guy you say got himself scragged, what was his name?'

'I don't recall.'

'We'll help you in a little while,' George assured me. I didn't like to hear it. 'And what makes you think Mrs. Proctor knows anything about it?'

I was puzzled by the way the Tuscanos were handling the situation. I knew their earlier histories, and even more important, I knew the type. Only too well. It was not a natural order of things for them to be sitting around, drinking my beer, and asking questions like lady reporters. I would have expected a more direct approach, like a quick going over, and a broken glass held at my throat. There was something here I didn't understand. When I don't understand things, it makes me nervous. Why didn't they cut out all this pussyfooting around, and just put the blast on me? That way, I would have understood.

'I've talked too much already. Don't want to make my throat sore,' I replied.

'You ain't talked at all,' snarled Al. 'But you will. O.K. now, George? We did it your way, and it didn't work, right? The guy wants to play it rough.'

'I'd have to go along with brother Al, if we're voting.'

Tony may talk a little smoother than the other two, but it was only the smoothness of a finer glasspaper. Underneath he was just as rough. George nodded.

'Pity. I would have done it nice, if we could.'

I got up, then. Whatever was going to

happen, it wasn't going to start off with me sitting down.

The door buzzer sounded.

We froze where we were. George Tuscano made a clucking sound.

'You expecting company?'

I nodded.

'It's a man with a gun,' I said, grave-faced.

'Yes it is,' scoffed Al. 'Most likely the laundry.'

'Or some dame,' supplemented Tony.

George jerked his head.

'Get rid of 'em, Tony.'

Tony went to the door and opened it, just a crack. There was a voice from outside.

'He ain't here right now,' said Tony. 'Come back in an hour.'

The door flew open, and Sam Thompson came marching in, a big revolver looking almost like a toy in that huge paw. He beamed around at the assembled company.

'A party,' he marvelled. 'A party with beer, and you tried to keep me out. Shame on you, Preston.'

I was going to have to revise my mental image of Thompson, I realised. Standing there, waving artillery at the invaders, he really made a very handsome picture.'

'Who is this clunk?' snarled George.

'Clunk?' Sam wrinkled his eyebrows. 'Is that polite?'

I chuckled with relief.

'No it isn't. These guys ought to be grateful to you, Sam. I was just about to beat 'em up.'

He swivelled heavy eyes around.

'All three at once?' he questioned.

'It wouldn't have been even, otherwise.'

'You always was one for the odds. Do they have names?'

'Just the one,' I told him. 'It's Tuscano.'

He studied each face in turn, nodding.

'The Tuscanos, huh? The only people I ever knew by that name was the Flying Tuscanos. Aerialists. Great act. Somehow, I don't think you're them.'

'And your name, clunk? What would that be?' hissed George.

Thompson ignored him.

'There he goes, with that clunk again. Ain't very sociable, is he?'

'It doesn't matter. This circus was just leaving anyway,' I announced.

George gave the smallest of nods, and the three brothers moved for the door.

'This time you got lucky, Preston,' he warned. 'There'll be other times.'

Al made no comment, but the glower on his face was enough. Tony waved his beer can at me.

'O.K. to take this with me?' he asked cheerfully. 'It's still half-full.'

There was something about Tony, a kind of infectious boyishness, that kept shoving its way through the tough guy exterior. You couldn't help grinning at the man.

'Be my guest,' I replied. 'This is drinking weather, not fighting weather.'

'We'll see,' he chuckled.

Then they were gone. Sam followed them outside, waited until they got into the elevator, then came back.

'What was all that about?' he demanded.

'I'll tell you later. First of all, thanks for showing when you did.'

'You knew I was coming,' he objected.

'Yes. But the timing was immaculate. Get yourself a drink Sam, and tell me what you found out.'

The tension was going out of me, and I began to feel deflated. My rescuer came back in with a tall glass, and stretched out in the chair Al Tuscano had just vacated.

'Mud,' he announced, taking a deep pull.

I nodded, leaning back and setting fire to an Old Favorite.

'Did you check on that party?'

'Yup. Kind of disappointing, it was. I'd been hoping for some kind of call-girl, or an actress or whatever. Nothing like that.'

'Now we know what you didn't find, maybe you'll tell me what you did.'

'Kay.' He pulled a piece of paper from his pocket, and squinted at it. 'Iris Moorland is twenty-seven years old. She is the assistant librarian out at the County Hospital. That's like a special kind of library, you know? I mean it's not just any old books. It's all this medical stuff, and to be a librarian you have to pass all kinds examinations, and like that. Way I been hearing it, you got to be more of a doctor yourself before you get the job.'

I listened carefully.

'I know what you mean. So our Iris is kind of bright. What else?'

'She's been at the hospital two, maybe three years. I don't know where she was before that, on account of I didn't have the time. We can get to it later, if you want.'

'Maybe. What kind of gal is she?'

He shifted around, and the chair protested.

'Didn't get to see her, not yet. Way I hear it, she's a neat dresser, no great shakes as a looker. Doesn't seem to laugh a lot, or have much to say for herself. Spends all her free time with her daughter, the kid is two years old by the way, and does a little community work at the weekend. The house is in good shape, from the outside anyway.'

Sam had been busy.

'What about the husband, what does he do?'

He scratched thoughtfully at his chin.

'Little bit of a query mark, there. She calls herself Mrs. Moorland, but there isn't any husband around. Everybody seems to think he's probably dead. She never talks about him.'

I objected.

'Dead? Why does he have to be dead? Why

96

couldn't they be divorced, or separated?'

'I don't know,' he replied, in a hurt tone. 'I'm only passing on gossip. Fact is, this Iris Moorland is what you might call kind of a reserved party. Keeps herself to herself, pays her dues, dotes on this daughter, makes sure everything is nice and orderly. A good citizen, all around.'

A good citizen all around. Why would such an all around good citizen get her name in the pocket of a man who'd been shot to death? Without much hope, I said,

'You don't think there's a possibility our Iris is kidding everybody? You know the kind of thing. Gets home from the hospital in the evening, takes off the hornrim glasses, and becomes Lulu, the darling of the night spots?'

Sam yawned.

'No dice. I don't believe she's the brains behind all these armed stickups we've been getting. You read too many newspapers, Preston. And you didn't take a ride out to this New Monastery Drive. I did. Believe me, it's the kind of neighborhood, you raise your voice to your dog, there's a protest to the Animal Cruelty squad the next morning. Just last week, a guy was fifteen minutes late getting back from the office. They're still talking about it. That's the kind of environment it is. The international vice ring is out.'

Pity. I'd been hoping for more. Iris Moorland had seemed like a gift-wrapped key to some part of this puzzle. It began to look as though Gus Brasselle had been wasting his time, too.

'So what happens next?' demanded Thompson. 'You want me to waste some more of your money on this girl?'

'No,' I decided. 'Not right now. Maybe later. I have to make a call in a few minutes. We'll fill in the time talking about the Tuscanos.'

'Good. They seem like the kind of people I ought to know more about.'

I began to bring him up to date.

CHAPTER SEVEN

When Thompson had left, it was time for my contact with Shoemaker. He picked up the phone on the second buzz, and we went through that wailing tone routine again.

'You ought to get that thing patented,' I suggested.

'It's been filed,' he assured me. 'What developments have you to report? I heard about the murder of that man on the car radio.'

'The news is the usual mixture,' I told him. 'The good side of it is that the manager of the apartment-house is a man with an eye to the dollar. He didn't tell the police about me, so to that extent I'm still ahead.'

98

'You've talked with him, then?'

'Couple of hours ago. The reason he kept quiet is that he thinks he can make a score. This is the hard part, Mr. Shoemaker. He wants ten thousand dollars.'

He took in breath sharply.

'That's a great deal of money. Why does he think you might pay him a sum like that? Does he think you—er—were responsible for what happened?'

'No. As a matter of fact, even if he were to tell what he knows about me, it would only confirm that I couldn't have done it. The victim had been dead for some time before I arrived. His testimony would only corroborate that.'

'Then there has to be something else.'

'Right. The manager knows something. I don't know what it is, but he thinks it's worth ten coarse notes. He also says he has one other place he could go to sell his information. I have until ten o'clock this evening to make good.'

There was a pause while Shoemaker digested this.

'Not very satisfactory is it? I mean you don't even know what you'll be buying. Assuming you buy anything at all. We haven't agreed that yet. What do you imagine it can be?'

I'd had a while to think about that one.

'I make it one of two things. One is that he knows a certain lady is involved. I don't say guilty, just involved. If that's the case, then he could be thinking that she would be willing to pay that kind of money to be kept out of it. Either herself, or some member of the family might be willing to pay.'

'H'm. What's the other possibility?'

'The other one is that the man knows something much bigger. Something which is going on, and which the investigator was working on when he was murdered. He already hinted to me that he was in Brasselle's confidence. They were cousins, it seems.'

'Which of those alternatives do you prefer?'

'I like the second one better. I get a feeling there is something afoot. Just what it is, and who fits where, these are things I don't know yet. But it seems to me that if some third party might be willing to pay ten thousand dollars for it, then it won't be to keep a certain lady's name out of the newspapers.'

More silence. Then,

'I don't know that I necessarily agree. This talk about a third party could be no more than bluff.'

I made contradictory noises.

'I don't think so. This man is convinced that what he has is hot merchandise. He intends to leave town when he collects his money. He's scared too. Just wants to collect, and blow. That's why he gave me the deadline.'

'You have until ten o'clock, you say?'

'Correct.'

'Very well. What is your recommendation? When I hire a man, I hire his judgement as well. Do you think we should pay?'

That, as they say, was the sixty-four dollar question. Or, more precisely, the ten thousand dollar question.

'Let me put it this way. There are several hours between now and pay-off time. I shan't be wasting them. But I think I ought to be in a position to pay the man, if there's no alternative. Can you raise the money at this time of evening?'

'Yes.'

'Then I suggest you do it. I won't part with your cash if there's any way I can avoid it, and you can believe I'll be trying. But, when I think of your own position, and this kind of publicity, I have to say ten thousand dollars is a small item.'

'All right, I will arrange for the money to be available. I have an official engagement this evening, so I can't speak with you again. How will you collect the cash?'

M'm. If I was going to be chasing around town, it would only hamper me to be in a certain place at a certain time.

'Do you know the Oyster's Cloister?'

'Naturally.'

Naturally, I sighed. The Cloister is the most expensive eating-house within twenty miles.

'The owner, Reuben Krantz, he's a friend of mine. Have the money left with him.'

101

His tone was guarded when he asked,

'Will that be—um—satisfactory?'

'If you mean will Ben Krantz hook on to your cash, you can forget it.'

'That wasn't entirely what I meant. It's the connection between us that worries me. I don't wish to draw attention to it.'

'No need for you or your name to be involved. Just have the parcel left there, to be collected by me, and no one else.'

'If you think it's safe.'

'I know it is. One last thing, I'd feel happier about things if I could report what's been going on, before you go to bed. Is there any chance of our talking, late tonight?'

'Hold on, I'll have to look at some papers.'

I inspected the wall. The trouble with making calls from your own joint is the lack of artwork on the walls. In a public booth, I would have been able to catch up on some reading.

'Are you still there?'

'Right here.'

'Well, I could be near this number from eleven forty five until midnight. I'm sorry it's tight, but I have a milk-and-biscuits conference at twelve fifteen. A new party idea, to demonstrate how sober we all are at that hour.'

Great. I never had any political ambitions anyway. This latest crazy notion only confirmed my thinking.

'All right, Mr. Shoemaker, I'll try to call within those fifteen minutes.'

We broke the connection. I was about to walk out when I changed my mind, and looked up Angela Proctor's number. The phone rang a long time before she answered.

'Mrs. Proctor?'

'Who is this?'

Her voice was low, almost as if she didn't want some third party to hear what she was saying.

'I was out at the house earlier,' I reminded. 'I give swimming lessons, and elementary wrestling.'

'Oh it's you. What do you want?'

'I want to finish our conversation. The one we were having before your little playmate arrived.'

She didn't reject the idea immediately, which was a good sign.

'I don't think we have anything to talk about,' she demurred.

A time-gainer.

'You're very wrong about that. There's trouble about, a whole flock of trouble. Just how far you're involved, I don't know. It could be simply a matter of getting your name splashed around in the newspapers again. Or it could be very much more. Like personal danger.'

'I think you're being dramatic.'

'It won't do, Mrs. Proctor. You don't believe

that for a minute. If you did, you'd have told me to go peddle my papers, and slammed down the phone. I want to see you, and quick.'

'How long will it take?' She'd already forgotten she wasn't interested.

'That will depend on how long you spend time pussyfooting around, and dodging questions. Could be ten minutes, only.'

'Do you want to come here?'

I chuckled.

'No, I don't think so. You have the strangest line in house guests. How about meeting me in the car park outside City Hall? This time of evening, the place is deserted.'

'I really don't see—' she began.

'I think you do, Mrs. Proctor, and we're wasting time.'

If she weren't such a good-looking gal, I would have described the sound that followed as a snort.

'Twenty minutes, then?'

'See you there.'

The now-familiar M.G. was there ahead of me. From two hundred available spaces, Angela Proctor had selected the one at the foot of the City Hall steps. The one marked plainly 'Reserved for Mayor'. She would. I moved into the subsidiary role of City Treasurer, and got out of the car. She rolled down her window and inspected me.

'Well, I'm here. What happens now?'

'We talk. Your boyfriend came to see me, by

the way. I was disappointed. I kind of had the impression you didn't want me involved in whatever all this is.'

By using the term boyfriend, I was being deliberately vague. Al Tuscano had arrived at her house as though he knew his way around. But the man who'd been her escort the previous evening had been his brother George. I didn't know who fitted where.

'Boyfriend?'

'Tuscano.'

'He's not my boyfriend. He—well, that doesn't matter. What happened?'

'What happened was my place was full of Tuscanos. They came there to play rough. Would have done it too, but a friend of mine arrived. He showed them a line of reasoning they couldn't argue against.'

'Reasoning?' she repeated doubtfully.

'Yes. An eight-shot automatic pistol. That is a very powerful line of reasoning when you're dealing with people like that. The point is, why?'

'Why what?'

I made a face of annoyance.

'Look, we're not going to get anywhere if you just keep on looking poker-faced all the time. You know damn well why what. I want to know why those guys should care if I talk with you. I want to know what makes it any of their put-in. I want to know what is the connection between them and you. I want to know an awful lot of things, Mrs. Proctor.'

'Why should I tell you anything at all?' she said haughtily.

I sighed.

'We went through that already, back at your house. That's kind of a poor memory you have there. About poor old Gus Brasselle getting himself knocked off, and everything.'

She seemed to come to some kind of decision.

'Get in the car,' she commanded. 'I don't like looking up at you all the time.'

'Right.'

I would have to walk around the front. As I moved, the wing-mirror suddenly dissolved into flying fragments, and something metallic made a pinging sound off the marble steps to my left. I dived over the bonnet of the car, wrenched open the passenger door, and hurled myself inside.

'What did you do to the mirror?' she demanded. 'And what's all the—?'

'Start driving, lady. That was a gunshot. Somebody doesn't like us.'

At least she didn't argue, she backed around hurriedly, and we leaped forward as she jammed her foot down. I was peering out into the gloom, in the vague direction from which the shot must have come. A thirty eight was in my hand, but it was more in reflex than from any thought that it would be of any use.

'Where to?'

'Just out of here. There's an all-night garage two blocks east. We'll go there, for a start.'

'Can you see anything?'

My head was screwed right round, as I stared behind us.

'Nothing.'

She turned expertly out of the parking area at speed, and I breathed noisily.

'You know, Mrs. Proctor, you really are going to have to talk to me, before we all get dead.'

'H'm. I didn't hear any shot.'

'Neither did I,' I confirmed. 'But I heard what happened when that slug hit the steps. And you saw what it did to the mirror. That was a rifle, lady. A high-powered rifle, plus silencer.'

'Do you think they'll come after us?'

'No. You can ease up on the speed.'

She wasn't convinced.

'What makes you so positive?'

I took one final look out of the rear window, then relaxed. It seemed like a suitable time for a lecture in small-arms.

'The weapon,' I explained, 'You see, a rifle requires room before you can use it. Room, and a steady firing platform. You can't get either of those things in an automobile, chasing around at forty miles per hour. It also requires two hands. It isn't like a pistol, something you can shoot off anywhere, any time. No, we won't be chased. Besides, if the guy is all that anxious to kill us, he must know who we are. He can catch up with us later.'

She shivered.

'You're not a very comfortable person to be with,' she grumbled.

'Maybe not, but I'll tell you this.' I watched her face. 'It's more comfortable sitting here than lying on the next slab to old Gus, down at the city morgue.'

She bit hard at her lip.

'Is that the garage you meant?'

A lighted forecourt loomed ahead.

'That's the one. Pull in there, please.'

I climbed out of the car, and went into a huddle with the night manager. When I got back to Angela Proctor, she had suffered some kind of reaction. One of her hands was clenched tightly round the wheel, and in the other was a lighted cigaret, which she attacked with short, stabbing puffs. There was strain on her face.

Sliding in beside her, I said gently,

'You were pretty good, back there. It's a kind of relief to see that you're not really made of steel.'

She nodded, without replying. We sat quietly for a few moments, then she shuddered, drew in a deep breath, and leaned her head back.

'I'm sorry about that.'

The voice was small.

'There's no need. Most women would have

collapsed on the spot, and left me to get on with it. Believe me, I know.'

Her eyes were grateful.

'I know that's not true, but thanks anyway. What are we doing here, Mr. Preston?'

It was nice to be promoted to the Mr. category.

'My car,' I explained. 'Our friend Hawkeye is probably back there, waiting for me to collect it. All he has to do is sit in the dark, and blow my head off when I show. I don't see why I should let him spoil my nice head. It's the only one I have. These guys,' I jerked a thumb towards the night depot, 'will pick it up, and deliver it back to my place.'

She had an immediate objection.

'Then all he has to do is to follow. They will lead him straight to where you live.'

I nodded.

'I don't think that matters too much. It's my guess he already knows who I am, anyway. Whatever you may read in the papers, people who shoot other people usually know who they are. No, the thing that is bothering me is, why? There's something big here. Something important enough to justify having me bumped off. So they must think I know something, or I'm on to it, one way or another. The fact is, I don't. And I'm not. If you see what I mean.'

I turned to look into her face. Her eyes were clouded now, and troubled, but she said nothing.

'I'm not going to get too excited, just because somebody took a shot at me. It's been done before. But I like to know why.'

She wagged her head, then seemed to change the subject.

'If your car is being taken to where you live, hadn't I better drive you there? While we're waiting, we could talk.'

It sounded like an offer.

'Will I learn anything?' I demanded.

'Yes. I think it's about time.'

'Then let's go.'

CHAPTER EIGHT

She stood in the doorway of the apartment at Parkside, and looked around. I'd seen the look before on women visitors' faces. They always want to know what kind of place a man runs, what state it's in. Their beady little eyes are watching out for piles of dirty laundry, garbage all over the floor. General signs of neglect, just because there isn't any female on the premises. It goes against their instincts and training to imagine that a man without a female can live in anything but squalor.

'The rest of the place is tidy, too,' I assured her. 'You can inspect it later.'

'I'm sorry, I didn't mean to stare,' she mumbled, coming in and closing the door.

'They always do. Please sit down. Can I get you a drink?'

'Er no. No thank you. This is really very nice.'

What she meant was, how could I afford it?

'I'm an expensive man to hire,' I told her. 'When I've had a hard day, tossing guys into pools and being shot at, I like to come back to a little comfort.'

She smiled then.

'You certainly have it here. You must be rather good, Mr. Preston.'

I kept a straight face.

'I'm not merely good, Mrs. Proctor. I am absolutely the best in the business. You want to hear about my day? Better say yes, because I'm going to tell you anyway.'

She made a face.

'In that case, yes. Please.'

I lit a cigaret, and sat down.

'This morning, I found a dead man. He was your man. I went to see a lady, and a gangster turned up at the house. Your house. Next I had a blackmail offer, details to follow. Three guys came here to work me over. Your guys. I went to meet a lady, and somebody took a shot at me. The lady was you.'

Angela sat quite still as I went through the lovely chronicle. I jabbed the Old Favorite towards her.

'I may have been kidding just now, when I said I was the best in the business. But it doesn't need any great brain power for a man to work out that the one constant factor in everything that happens is you. Now do you feel like talking?'

'Do I have a choice?'

'Very little.'

'No. I can see that I haven't. We shall have to start with my husband. Do you know anything about him?'

I tried to recall the very little I'd heard.

'Doctor Edwin Proctor, age around forty two, forty three—'

'Forty two.'

'Right. Married once before, widowed. Some kind of specialist—'

'Consultant. Consultant in recuperative medicine,' she interjected.

'That means what? That he specialises in nervous disorders, stuff like that?'

'That is the field in which he is most prominent,' she confirmed. 'Or was. But he feels that medical people generally ought to keep in touch with routine medicine. He always maintained that a doctor can get caught up in some narrow field, to the degree where he loses all contact with the rough and tumble of general practise. Too busy making a living, as he used to say, and forgetting about being a doctor. And so, two days each week, he worked at the County Hospital. To keep himself in touch with reality, as he put it, and to keep abreast of modern technological

112

advances.'

If you want to make any progress in my dodge, you have to learn to listen. It's a special kind of listening. Some people think it's a simple matter of taking in words which are being spoken by someone else, and that's all. That isn't all. Words are important, it's true. Equally important is inflection, the look on people's faces, and even the way they hold themselves while uttering. A lot of the time, these things say as much as the words, and sometimes more.

Take, for example, the way Angie Proctor was talking about her husband. There was pride in her voice when she spoke. That, and a touch of affection, and something else. Wistfulness? She was sitting very straight in her chair, a half-smile on her face, and looking, not at me, but at some point in the middle distance. Whatever caused them to split up, it hadn't been hatred, or contempt. Not on her part, anyway. There was one other thing, and that puzzled me. She kept on referring to the man in the past tense.

It was something I had to know more about.

'Mrs. Proctor—' I began.

'Hadn't we better drop the formalities?' she suggested calmly. 'Most of the people who join me in target practise call me Angie.'

I smiled. A cool one, this.

'Angie, then. The other targets call me Mark.'

'I know.'

'About your husband. You have used the past tense a number of times in the last few minutes. A slip of the tongue?'

She frowned a little.

'You don't know about Edwin?'

I shook my head.

'Only more or less what you've been telling me up to now. And you don't live together. I know that much.'

She smiled then. It was a lop-sided, wry kind of expression.

'I was brought up to believe it's a sign of weakness to admit error. You called me a rich-bitch this afternoon—oh, it's all right, I'm not going to start a fight. I was being high hat, and generally insufferable, and you were just hitting back. Actually, it wasn't too far from the truth. I've done pretty much whatever I choose, ever since I was about four years old. Edwin Proctor was a new experience for me. A brilliant mind, and I could respond to that without wondering why. But as a man, he was a simple, uncomplicated person, who loved me totally. It was altogether strange, something I'd never encountered before. I haven't been exactly a protected rose all my life, as you must know, but this man was altogether different. I was not prepared for him, emotionally prepared, that is. I became frightened and worried, didn't think I could cope with the situation. So I left him.'

114

She was only half-talking to me. For the rest, she was thinking out loud. There are times when the listener doesn't interrupt. This was one of those times. After a pause, she continued.

'When I say I left him, I don't mean there was a great flaming row, or anything of that kind. It was one afternoon. Edwin was away, and I was alone in the house, trying to clear my mind, to adjust to this entirely new man–woman relationship. To me, it was all so strange, that I should feel calm and contented. Not waiting for the next expedition into lion-country. Just happy with things the way they were. It was typical of me that I should react the way I always have. If I'm upset or troubled, I just take off. That's what I did. I thought I'd get away by myself, just for a few weeks. It would give me time to get the marriage into perspective. Naturally, the news-hounds didn't bother with my motives, not that I'd have told them anyway. It was just another Angela story to them. I'd acted up before, and here I was, acting up again. But they were wrong, this time.'

Her voice trailed away, and I waited. But she'd vanished into her own thoughts this time.

'But that was over a year ago,' I prompted softly. 'You've had time to come to some kind of decision.'

She started, as though I'd made an unwelcome interruption.

'Eighteen months, actually. And you're right, of course. I came to a decision very quickly. I wanted everything the way it was. The marriage, and life together, everything. I was all set to move back to the house when the accident happened.'

My puzzlement was genuine.

'Accident?'

'You sound as if you don't know about it. Edwin was leaving the hospital. It was late afternoon. He was walking to his car, when he was run down by another car that had gone out of control. It was in all the papers.'

It's always difficult for people who are involved in things, to understand why the uninvolved don't remember every little paragraph in the newspapers. Particularly after such a long time.

'I must have read about it at the time.'

'It didn't seem particularly serious at first, not much more than a glancing blow. Edwin suffered a few bruises and abrasions. He was unconscious of course, but they assured me at the hospital that once he recovered, he'd be able to leave. A couple of days rest would put him back on his feet.'

There was bitterness in her voice now. I waited to learn why.

'They were right, in a sense. He was back on his feet quite quickly. What they hadn't been able to foresee was the damage to his brain. He'd struck his head when he fell, and it left

116

him a vegetable. A walking dead man. He had no memory worth speaking of. It took him six months to learn how to eat his food. He lives in a home now. It's a good place, and he's quite happy there, but to all intents and purposes, he's dead. I'm one of his favorite people, did you know that? I'm the nice lady who always brings him candy.'

Her voice was half-strangled as she uttered the last words. I was afraid she might break down on me. The floor covering is a mottled brown weave, alternate light and dark shades, and I studied it carefully for signs of wear. There was silence for a moment, then she laughed. A short, brittle sound.

'Don't look so worried, Mark. I'm not going to throw a fit on you. I've had quite a time to adjust.'

I looked at her then.

'You also had quite a situation to adjust to.'

'Thank you. Yes, I did. At first, I didn't believe it. Things like that just didn't happen to me. They were not permitted to happen. Everything always went the way I wanted it to. I always got my own way. If I couldn't charm my way through, then I would bulldoze. If I couldn't bulldoze, then I would buy. Money has never been any problem, as you must know. This accident of Edwin's brought an entirely new concept. But not for some time. Months, in fact. There had to be something that could be done. Someone who could put him right. I scoured the world, and that is no more than the literal truth. There must be a doctor somewhere, a brain surgeon, who would be able to operate. It took a long time for me to accept that this was one situation I wasn't going to be able to beat. That was a bad time.'

It was costing her quite an effort to tell me all this. Some people bleed easily. They can pour out all their troubles to anyone who happens to be handy. A neighbor, a bartender, a fellow-passenger on a bus ride. Other people can't do it. They keep everything bottled up inside. Angie Proctor was one of those.

'I'm not too well-informed, medically,' I told her. 'Exactly what kind of damage did your husband suffer? Was it some destruction of the actual brain tissue, or what?'

She shook her head.

'Oh no. That was what used to infuriate me. It's something very small. Some particle of foreign matter which is lodged somewhere at the base of the brain. If it were anywhere else, an operation would be possible. No guarantee of success, you understand, but it would be possible to try. But this thing is inaccessible. One day, it could happen that the obstruction could be dislodged naturally. A sudden jerk might shift it. Anything. But so far as human intervention is concerned, it's out of the question.'

'Then we can only hope.'

I thought it was time to get off the subject.

She smiled gratefully.

'Imagine me, telling you all that. You're a good listener, aren't you?'

'I try to break up my day,' I said, straight-faced. 'So much time for tossing people into pools, so much for being shot at, so much for listening.'

It was a deliberate attempt to snap her out of it, and I got my reward. A low, lazy chuckle.

'I know what you're doing, and thank you. Don't worry, I was about to put the violin back in its case.'

'I didn't mean—'

'It's all right. I've done my weeping. Time to get back to the present.' Her voice now was brisk, and the sadness had left it. 'Well, after I reached the point where I knew it was hopeless, I had to decide what I was going to do with my life. It seemed obvious, once I had my thinking straight. What I had to do was to carry on in Edwin's place, in those areas where I was capable. I'm no doctor, so all the medical side was out of the question. But he also was a champion of Ad-Hoc, you know, the children's organisation? Edwin was one of the original members of the founding committee. It wasn't just a question of allowing people to put his name on the notepaper. He really was interested, and did quite a lot of work, particularly in the early days.'

'Why do you put it like that?' I questioned.

119

'Do you imply that his interest had been getting less?'

A shake of the head.

'Oh no, I didn't mean that at all. But you know the way things are, when there's something new to be set up. It means a lot of work for a few dedicated people. Ideas have to be hardened, translated into practical working form. Money has to be raised, organisation created. These things take a lot of time, and hard work. If the desired results are achieved, then the ideas become realities. The blueprint becomes a building, with a work force and a working program. A point is reached where the goal has been achieved. That is the way it was with Ad-Hoc. It is now a recognised organisation, with funds and staff. There is no longer the pressure on Edwin and the others to give so much of their personal time. The initial job was done. The work, naturally, goes on. Probably for as many years ahead as anyone can foresee. And that's where I was able to come in.'

I had been paying careful attention.

'I'm with you. You could give your time to the organisation, carry on with the work Edwin had started.'

'Exactly. Not at any very high level, of course. Office routine, meetings, things like that. But I'm not entirely without brains. Plus, I'm a willing worker, and I'm free. That alone saves several thousand dollars a year. I think it's worthwhile.'

'I think it's admirable,' I volunteered, and I meant it. 'And it keeps the Proctor name alive in the organisation.'

'I like to think so.'

Everything was getting so cosy around here, it seemed a pity to introduce anything sordid. But it must be done.

'It all seems a far cry from gunshots and murder.'

She shook her head rapidly, and blinked.

'That was quite a switch,' she accused.

'It was necessary,' I assured her. 'I have to see a man before ten o'clock tonight, so I don't have a lot of time. I've no idea what he's going to tell me, or even what it will mean. But you could be affected—'

'Me?'

'—yes. And on top of that, there's another guy out there with a rifle. He seems to want to kill me, and again, I'm in the dark as to why. There are things you know, Angela, and I am going to have to be told. I've worked in the dark before, but it seems ridiculous to have to do it, when you could throw some light around.'

'Yes.' She chewed at her lower lip, thinking. 'This man you have to see. Why should that involve me?'

'Because I think he's going to be able to tie you in with Gus Brasselle. I also think, in fact he told me so, that he's considering selling this

121

information to other people.'

'What other people? Who'd be interested?'

'I don't know.'

'And you used the word "sell". Do you mean this is a blackmail situation?'

'That's exactly what I mean. Oh, you don't have to worry about that angle. Nobody's going to shake you down, if that's what you're thinking.'

She flushed at that.

'I'm sorry, I'm a little confused. I shouldn't have suggested—Will you forget I said that?'

'Gladly. But it won't change things. I still have to know whatever it is that you know. And you'd better start with the dead man, Brasselle. You will notice, by the way, that I'm taking it for granted you didn't kill him yourself.'

Angie Proctor had quite recovered her composure now, and she looked at me warily.

'You think that's a safe assumption? I have a gun.'

'You, and ten million other people in this country. But all right, I'll ask you the question. Did you bump off this Brasselle?'

'No, I did not.'

'So maybe we can pick it up from there. What, as they say, is the story?'

She smoothed the stray hair away from her eyes.

'Is there a drink? This may take a while.'

CHAPTER NINE

Strictly speaking, my apartment at Parkside is designed and adapted for solo living, but I had to admit Angie Proctor was an improvement. Sitting there, with her knees folded decorously sidewise on the davenport, and a tinkling glass in her hand, she made a handsome picture. I'm not normally one for re-runs, but it was a picture I could sit through any number of times over.

'All right lady, we have our drinks. The floor is yours.'

The floor, yes. Also the walls, the ceiling, the furnishings, and anything else she took a shine to. She wasn't flirting with me, exactly. It's just that some dames have a way with them. But when she spoke, her voice was serious, and low.

'About ten days ago, a man came to see me. He said his name was Gus Brasselle, and that he was a private investigator. He had a proper license and everything. Official State of Texas stamps, and so forth. I looked at it with great care, believe me.'

I looked surprised.

'Really? Why? It's my experience that I simply wave my I.D. around, and most people take it as read.'

She licked at the immaculate teeth, and

almost looked shy.

'I imagine they do. The trouble is, in my case, I've had more than my share of badges and warrants over the years. It has been necessary for me to learn, after some earlier experiences, exactly what powers can be exercised by exactly what people. When I tell you that I looked very hard, you can believe me.'

The reference was to her turbulent early years, and I was sorry it had to be made.

'Sorry,' I mumbled. 'I didn't mean to doubt you.'

'Anyway, this Mr. Brasselle needed some help. He was representing a family, he didn't tell me where they lived, but it had to be within reach of Dallas.'

'Why?'

'Because that's where he had his office,' she explained patiently.

'Oh.'

I didn't elaborate on the point. In present-day Texas, people think nothing of flying hundreds of miles, merely to do a little shopping in a great center like Dallas. Or maybe just for a luncheon appointment. 'Within reach' had little meaning.

'Well, as I say, he represented this family. They had adopted a small child through the organisation, through Ad-Hoc that is. The child is now two years old, and extremely happy. And healthy.'

She made the last part a separate statement. I looked at her with enquiry on my face.

'Yes,' she nodded, 'I'm going to explain that. This family had been approached by a man, a blackmailer. According to him, the child was one of a family. There were two others, a boy and a girl, it seems.'

That puzzled me.

'Sorry to interrupt, but I don't follow that. You say "it seems". I don't know from beans about the rules on the adoption business, but I thought all these things were made clear to prospective parents from the beginning.'

'Your thinking is correct,' she agreed, 'and as far as possible these things are done, as you say. But with these children, it isn't an easy matter. You must have some idea of the chaos out there across the Pacific. Sometimes a whole village arrives, sometimes just an ox-cart with one old lady and three or four children. There is no documentation of the various civilian populations, not in the neat, orderly fashion we understand. There are just people, in need of help. Even the language barrier is all but insurmountable, with many of the dialects involved. The so-called interpreters are often locals who have just enough pidgin English to understand bath houses, mealtimes, and blanket issues.'

Old, half-forgotten scenes flooded back into my memory.

'It's been a few years now, but I know what

you mean. You were telling me about this man, the one who said the adopted baby had a brother and sister somewhere. What was the point?'

'The point was that the sister had died. From a disease which is well-enough known in that particular country, but doesn't occur over here. The germ, apparently, can lie dormant for years. Then something resurrects it. No ordinary doctor would recognise the signs, not in the early stages. By the time it's obvious, it's too late. The patient is dead.'

'What's the name of the disease?'

Angie shook her head.

'That's the whole point. The man wouldn't tell. He wants fifty thousand dollars first.'

'Wow,' I whistled. 'That's a lot of money.'

'It doesn't worry them, it seems. They have plenty of money.'

'But just a moment. Surely all that is necessary is for the new parents to take their child to a specialist in tropical medicine? I'm sure we have many fine doctors in that—'

I stopped talking because she was smiling sadly.

'Oh yes. There are a number. That was the immediate reaction of the parents, and that's what they did. It seems that there are at least four known diseases in that category. The early treatment for each one is different. Worse than that, the early treatment for one disease could positively encourage and assist another, if it's the wrong diagnosis. Now you can see the problem.'

'The problem, yes. But not the method of dealing with it. If this story is true, why should Brasselle come to you? Why didn't he just march in through the front door of Ad-Hoc and demand to see the president of the corporation, or whatever?'

She sipped at her drink, and set it down beside her.

'Because the parents are afraid. Your question is the first one I asked Brasselle. He was rather evasive at first, but he could see I wasn't going to budge, without the truth. These people had jumped the queue. And I tell by your face I'm going to have to explain that.'

She was right.

'Please.'

'Ad-Hoc, and organisations like it, have enormous waiting lists of people anxious to adopt. It's not a simple question of baby-shopping. People are vetted thoroughly, backgrounds studied, and so forth. A lot of them are rejected, for one reason or another. Those who are considered to be suitable are placed in strict rotation. The number of children available for adoption, at any given time, falls far short of the numbers of prospective parents.'

'So these particular parents had got themselves promoted up the line,' I finished.

'Somebody, somewhere, took a handout.'

Angie sighed.

'I'm afraid it's not impossible. I've even had one or two rather obvious offers made to me, in the course of interviews. A thousand dollars, on one occasion.' Then, seeing my reaction, she added 'and you ought not to judge people too harshly. They don't want to wait a year, and possibly two or three years, before they can have their baby. As for the office staff, well, they're not all dedicated, you know. Most of them are simply skilled administrators, and the job is just like another. A thousand dollars can seem like a lot of money. They're not even doing anything illegal, not even undesirable. All they do is put an application file a drawer or two higher than it ought to be.'

Put like that, it didn't sound too bad.

'And the parents from Texas are scared that this might all come to light, and somebody will take their child away,' I mused.

'That's right. As for the approach to me, it's easily explained. Brasselle knew that I work there for nothing. That makes me a person dedicated to the work, someone who would probably have that extra bit of devotion to the children, which the paid staff wouldn't necessarily feel. Someone who wouldn't reveal the truth, and take a chance on spoiling the happiness of that little family over in Texas.'

'He was a good guesser, wasn't he?'

'I'm afraid he was. I have my hard spots, but

not where the children are concerned.'

I lit an Old Favorite, to cover an awkward moment.

'So, as I gather it, he wanted you to check the records, see if you could find out about this sister, the one who died?'

'Exactly. If I could trace the sister, find out who her new parents were, it would then be a simple matter to follow up. If the child had indeed died, then the cause of death could be determined, and the necessary medical precautions taken.'

'So you agreed to do it.'

I made it a statement.

'Yes I did,' she replied coolly. 'I've spent too much of my own life bucking the authorities to become all holy about other people's mistakes. And there was the life of a child involved. I didn't think it would make too much of a criminal of me, to take a look in a couple of files.'

It was clear from her tone that the subject wasn't open for argument, even if I wanted to give her one.

'What did you find? Was it true?'

She shrugged.

'I found it wasn't going to be quite as simple as it sounded. When I went to the record system, the papers were missing. They were on our red star system, and I don't normally have access.'

'You're going to have to explain that, I'm

129

afraid.'

'The baby was a survivor from the Newland Hope disaster. You must remember that. The immigration ship that caught fire just a few hours before it docked.'

That one I did remember. It had been, what, eighteen months earlier, perhaps two years. There had been sabotage on the ship, and there was danger the children would suffocate in the smoke. The local yacht boys had mounted a big rescue operation to get them ashore. It had been a tremendous story at the time. All the news media had played it up as a second Dunkirk, the time when the British sent their pleasure launches across the English Channel to rescue their army from Hitler. As it was, the operation wasn't a total triumph. Almost two hundred children were lost. But a thousand were saved, and this child Angie Proctor was talking about had been one of them.

'I remember it very well,' I agreed. 'Of course, I only read it, like any other member of the public. I hadn't any reason to take the kind of interest your organisation must have had.'

'No. Well, as you will recall, the small boats brought the children ashore. There was some kind of row aboard ship about the necessity. It seems the fires were under control, and the captain couldn't see any need for anyone to leave the ship. It was the doctor in charge who forced the issue. It wasn't fire he was

130

concerned about. It was the effects of all that smoke on the children. Babies, in fact, most of them. He was right, too. A number of them died, and it could have been a lot more, if they hadn't taken to the boats.'

'And didn't something happen to one of the boats?' I recalled.

'Yes. There was a collision or something. In all the smoke and confusion, it wasn't easy to establish exactly what happened. But one of the launches sank, and the crew and the children were all lost. It was a terrible tragedy.'

I was trying to recall the names of the men who died, but they escaped me at the time.

'A shocking business,' I agreed briskly, shaking her mind back to the present. 'But you were saying something about a red star system.'

She blinked rapidly a couple of times.

'Yes. The red star system. The children who survived the Newland Hope disaster were placed in a separate category for the purposes of our records. The paper work about them was scanty enough originally, and even some of that was lost in the fire. That meant almost entirely new documentation for quite a few of them, some of it little more than guesswork. Ad-Hoc felt, and the government agreed, that in the case of these particular children it was more important even than usual to safeguard their records. When they reach maturity there could be all manner of court proceedings.

Suits against the shipping line, the government, the occupying governments of their lands of origin. It wouldn't be the first time that kind of thing has happened, and the organisation thinks ahead.'

'So does Uncle Sam, by the sound of it. Thank you for the background. The upshot seems to be that the records of the particular child you were checking were out of your reach.'

When she replaced the glass on the table it was empty. I pointed to it enquiringly, but she wagged a finger.

'No thank you. The file wasn't entirely out of my reach. It was just that I could only get to it when other people were out of the office. I would have to wait for an opportunity. I explained this to Brasselle, told him it might be days before a chance came my way. He wasn't too concerned. He said a few days one way or the other could scarcely make any difference. So I waited. Then, yesterday afternoon, I got my chance. Everyone else was either missing, or at a meeting in the office. I went upstairs to the red star system. There was still no file on this particular child. At first I thought I must be looking in the wrong place. I checked everywhere. There was no doubt. There is no file on that child in the Ad-Hoc offices.'

'H'm. What do you suppose it means?'

'I don't know. I've racked my brains ever

132

since. But I didn't finish the story. As I told you, there was a suitable break for me to search for the file. But that was assuming I could lay hands on it easily. When it wasn't in its proper place, I forgot about the time element. Just as I had given up the search, one of the staff came back into the office, and saw what I was doing. It was a senior supervisor, a man named Jeff Stone. He asked what I was looking for, and I made up some story about mislaying a file. At first I thought he was satisfied, and I went back to my own office. After about ten minutes he came storming in. He was in quite a rage. He told me he'd checked through the red star system, and it was obvious I'd been snooping around. I was taken quite aback, because after all it's only a filing system. It isn't exactly the blueprint room in a missile unit. I told him so, and ordered him out until he could control himself. Strictly speaking, he could have told me to go to hell, as he's senior to me many times over. But when I get on my high horse, it usually has some effect—'

'—I can imagine—'

'—so he did go away. Thirty minutes later, he came back and apologised. He said the responsibility of that batch of records was very heavy, what with government agents from all kinds of departments continually raising questions. I was so relieved that he wasn't going to press for my details that I forgave him on the spot. After I left work, I telephoned Brasselle. He wouldn't talk on the phone. He wanted to meet me, but I had a date for dinner, so he said he'd come along afterwards. It was very late last night when he came to the house. I explained to him what had happened. At first he didn't seem to believe me. Kept on cross-examining me, like some trial lawyer, to see if I'd change my story. I hadn't anything to hide, of course, and he could see that, finally. Then he asked me a strange thing. He asked if I would stay off work today. He would probably want to talk to me urgently, and obviously he couldn't do it at the office. I wasn't very keen on the idea, but I was feeling bad about those poor people in Texas, and not being able to find the file and everything. I finally agreed that I would go to work late, say a couple of hours. That would give him plenty of time to say whatever he had to say. It seemed to satisfy him, and he went home.'

'Did he give any idea what it was he wanted?' I queried. 'I mean, why should it have to wait till this morning?'

'I gathered he wanted to contact some other people first.'

I knew what time Gus Brasselle had left her the previous night, but there seemed no reason to let her know that.

'Why couldn't he have called them then? From your home, I mean.'

Pretty girls shouldn't make faces. One day

134

the wrinkles will remain.

'It was after one o'clock in the morning.'

That checked. Good.

'Would you mind telling me what happened this morning?'

Her head moved decisively from side to side.

'Not this morning. Last night. Brasselle telephoned me. It was almost three a.m. and I wasn't very happy to be woken up. He said things were now urgent, and there was a lot he had to tell me. Would I go down to this apartment building—'

'—the Granville Apartments—'

'—yes, at eleven thirty this morning. I was too sleepy to argue with the man. I agreed to go. I would have agreed to anything, just so I could get back to sleep.'

'So you kept the appointment?' I encouraged. 'Did anyone else see you? The manager, or anyone?'

'I don't think, although yes. Wait a minute. There was a man in the lobby. He must have noticed me.'

If he was under one hundred years old, there'd be no doubt about that, I decided.

'What kind of a looking guy was he? Tallish, on the thin side, very straight-backed?'

Angie tried to remember.

'I didn't really notice. After all, I had no way of knowing he might become important.'

She was beginning to sound a little

aggrieved.

'So you went up to the apartment. What did you find?'

'I tapped at the door a few times, but no one answered. The door was slightly open. I went inside—and—and found him.'

'Found him doing what?'

Her face was shocked.

'He wasn't doing anything. He was dead, murdered.' Her hand shook slightly, as she drummed on a cushion.

'Did you touch anything?'

'No. Of course not. I just felt the most terrible fear and shock. I guess I just ran out, in a panic.'

I ran fingers over my chin.

'A few minutes later, I was there myself. Tell me, why didn't you call the police? After all, it was nothing to do with you.'

'But I did,' she exclaimed. 'Once I'd got away from the place, and calmed down. I stopped off at a pay-phone, and reported in.'

'But you didn't identify yourself,' I suggested.

'No. There was no point. I had nothing to tell them about the poor man's death. When you've had as much publicity as I have, especially the kind that I have, you don't go looking for any more.'

I acknowledged the truth of that.

'They almost caught me. They came in the front door of the place, as I left by the rear. It was close.'

'So you weren't able to discuss your business with him, either. You never did tell me what you wanted with him.'

'No, I didn't.' And I had no intention of starting. 'I found the name of a woman among his stuff. I just wondered whether it might mean anything to you.'

'You could always ask.'

'The name was Moorland. Iris Moorland.'

She went very pale, and I thought for a moment she might pass out. Then she sighed deeply, and visibly pulled herself together.

'You did say Iris Moorland?'

'Yes. It obviously means something.'

She nodded gravely. 'It's the name of the librarian at the County Hospital. She was the one driving the car when my husband was knocked over.'

CHAPTER TEN

We stared at one another without speaking for most of a minute.

The telephone shrilled. I picked it up.

'Preston?'

Ben Krantz's voice.

'Hallo Ben. Long time.'

'No see,' he agreed. 'Listen, this is a high-class restaurant I run here. I don't need extra business as a parcel-collecting agency.'

It would seem that Mr. Shoemaker had kept his word.

'Do me a favor Ben. Hang on to it for just a few minutes. I'll be right over to pick it up.'

My watch said it was nine thirty five. I'd been so engrossed in my talk with Angie Procter that I hadn't realised how the time was slipping away.

'How do I know it isn't one of these plastic bombs?' he demanded, in an aggrieved tone.

'Now now Ben, you know how I work. When I leave bombs, I don't tell people who they're from.'

'A few minutes, right?'

'Right. I owe you, Ben.'

'Damn right,' he grumbled, and broke the connection.

Angie Proctor hadn't taken her eyes off me. My mind was still trying to pigeon-hole all the information she'd given me. It would have to wait for the moment. Hubbard had given me a ten o'clock deadline before he intended to put his merchandise on the open market. I couldn't risk him doing that.

'Are we going somewhere?' she asked dully.

'Not "we",' I corrected. 'Me. I want you to stay here. I'm not at all sure just what all this is about, but one thing is quite clear. Somebody out there is playing for keeps. Whether he's trying to kill you or me, or for that matter both of us, I don't know. But I want you out of the

138

way for a while. You'll be safe here. Don't let anyone in. Not anyone.'

It was clear from her face I was going to get an argument.

'What do you think I am? Some kind of china doll? I am not going to sit here with my knitting, while everything happens outside.'

There was no time for gentle persuasion.

'You are going to do exactly what I tell you,' I assured her, nastily. 'Otherwise I'm going to lock you in a cupboard. What's it going to be?'

Her eyes were angry, as we stared each other out.

'How long will you be gone?' she demanded, in a sulky tone.

'An hour. Maybe less.'

'One hour. I'll stay here one hour.'

It was the best deal I was going to get.

'Right. Remember. The door stays locked.'

I left her then, and went out in a hurry. The night-garage people had done a good job. The car was even in its correct slot. Minutes later I pulled in outside the front entrance of the Oyster's Cloister. Biff, the doorman, came over to see who was breaking the rules.

'Oh, it's you, Mr. Preston. C'm now, you know you can't leave it here.'

'Just picking up a parcel, Ben.'

I was in and out under ten minutes, with a thick manila envelope stuck in a side pocket. Biff waved as I backed away and pointed the nose across town. When I reached the

Granville Apartments, there were several vacant slots outside the building. I drove past, and around the first corner before parking the car. No point in drawing special attention to my arrival. The lobby was empty, but the door beyond the little cubicle was clearly marked 'Manager'. I tapped at it quietly.

'Who is it?' whispered a voice on the other side, almost at once.

'Preston.'

There was the rattling of a chain, then the door swung open. I stepped inside, to see a large youngish man sprawled in a chair facing me. He was a stranger. So was the other man, the one who had opened the door and now closed it quickly behind me. There was no sign of the man I'd come to see. It seemed to be their turn to speak.

The character in the chair smiled pleasantly. He had nice even teeth, and a devil-may-care look about him.

'Good evening,' he greeted. 'Mr. Preston, did you say?'

'I'm Preston, yes. Who're you people?'

'George, old man, just see if our guest is carrying anything heavy, would you mind? It's too hot an evening for excess weight.'

He'd been watching too many British spy movies. Nobody talks that way. George ran knowledgeable hands around me from behind. I was glad I'd left the money in the car.

'There's a gun here,' he grunted, patting at

140

me.

'A gun, really?' Even-teeth sounded surprised. 'I wonder if it's anything like this one.'

He produced a blue-black nine millimetre automatic from the vastness of his rumpled jacket and pointed it at my middle, jerking it to indicate that I was to remove my own weapon. I did so, gingerly. This wasn't the time for any thirty-yard runs.

'Oh dear no. Quite different. Let old George have a look at it, would you mind?'

Old George took it away from me, grunted, and stuck it in his pocket. He'd moved to where I could get a proper look at him now. The sight wasn't encouraging. George was in his early thirties, dressed in a charcoal business suit, with a close-cropped hairstyle and a very clean shave. These two were a team; and a team I didn't particularly care to play against.

'Sit down, Mr. Preston, sit down. Might as well be comfortable.'

I squatted unhappily, on an upright wooden chair, saying nothing.

'Friend of Mr. Hubbard's, are you?'

'Not exactly,' I replied.

'Ah.' He waited for more. There wasn't any. 'Then what are you doing here, Mr. Preston? Exactly.'

The gun had disappeared now, and he seemed perfectly relaxed, spread out every which way over the furniture.

141

'I came to see Hubbard.'

'Yes, yes,' he clucked, 'but we'll have to know more than that, I'm afraid. Mr. Hubbard won't be receiving visitors for a while. We'll be doing that for him.'

'Look,' I said edgily, 'I don't know who you are, or what you're doing here. I came to see Hubbard. O.K. he's not here. I'll go away.'

'Ah no,' he shook his head regretfully. 'Can't be done, I'm afraid. Not until we know a little more. You see, Mr. Hubbard is in trouble. A great deal of trouble. With the federal government.'

He let me see his teeth again.

'Federal gov—' I began, and stopped. 'You mean you guys are some kind of cops?'

The open face took on a pained expression.

'Oh no, I don't think we'd like to be called that, do you George?'

'Absolutely not,' agreed George. 'Makes us sound so ordinary.'

'Exactly. Couldn't have put it better myself.' The china-blue eyes almost twinkled. 'An ordinary policeman could take you in for questioning—'

'—one phone call—' inserted George.

'—and keep you for twenty-four hours. By which time your lawyer—'

'—a crook—'

'—is in with that writ thing. What's the Latin, George?'

'—Hokus Pokus—'

142

'—Paul Muni in "Scarface"?'

'—correct. It ought to be Hanky Panky—'

'—and there you are. Free. That's what your ordinary policeman can do,' concluded Eventeeth.

'It's very limiting,' added George nastily.

'Very. Now with us, you see, it's different. We can keep people weeks—'

'—months—'

'—and not a murmur to a living soul. Do you begin to follow us, Preston?'

I nodded sourly.

'I'm ahead of you. What happened to democracy?'

George snorted in disgust. The man in the chair beamed.

'You've upset George. That's a very sore point with him. Every little two-bit agitator, anyone who spends his life trying to undermine lawful government, starts shouting democracy when the government bites back.'

And now, for the first time since entering the room, I began to be afraid. If these guys were the real thing, I could be in a whole lot of trouble. Big trouble. I held up a hand.

'If you'll cut out the fancy banter, and talk a little plain English, we might make some progress. I'm not going to say you don't scare me. You do. You scare the hell out of me. But all this stuff about the government is way over my head. I'm not going to hold out on you. I'll tell you everything I can, if you're really

143

Washington people. But first, you have to show me.'

They exchanged a quick glance. George shrugged. The seated man reached inside his coat and pulled out a slim black-leather fold. Leaning forward, he opened it for me to see.

'I'm John L. Fisher, Bureau of Immigration.'

The card agreed with him. George leaned over my shoulder. His leather was brown, and the card was a different shape.

'George Cohen,' he announced. 'Maritime Commission.'

I looked carefully at both I.D.s. They hadn't been delivered with the breakfast cereal.

'All right,' I said resignedly, 'that's a lot of weight you're carrying. But I'm out of my depth here. What can I do for you people?'

Fisher put his identification away.

'You can start by telling us who you are, and what you want with Hubbard.'

'I'm a private investigator. Hubbard offered to sell me some information. I came to check it out.'

George Cohen was now standing where I could see him.

'With a thirty eight?' he asked softly. 'You always do your checking with a thirty eight?'

'I have a proper license for the gun. And when I'm toting money around, it makes me feel more comfortable.'

'Money?' interjected Fisher. 'I don't see

144

any. Is it hidden in your shoe?'

'It's in my car. In my experience, people get very edgy around money. This Hubbard might have taken it into his head to grab the money, and forget to give me the information. I've heard of it happening.'

'How much money?'

'Ten thousand.'

Fisher whistled softly.

'That much money? I think we'd better hear more about this valuable information.'

I took a pack of Old Favorites from my pocket, and lit one. Nobody tried to stop me. These two men weren't fooling around, and I was going to have to talk to them. There wasn't any reason why they shouldn't be told all the facts I had, such as they were. The difficult part was going to be in finding an explanation as to what made any of it my concern. Why was I involved in the first place? Federal men or not, I wasn't going to mention Mr. Shoemaker. The man could find himself in the middle of some congressional inquiry, or something of the kind. The newsboys would declare a holiday, and his enemies would probably name me Man of the Month.

'Don't waste too much time on it,' said Fisher.

I looked at him with my injured citizen expression.

'You'll have to explain that.'

'He means editing your scripts,' explained

Cohen. 'We're ready for the first pack of lies right now.'

'So if you wouldn't mind,' prompted his fellow-tormentor, 'just let it all hang out.'

I let out a small sigh.

'It starts with a guy by the name of Gus Brasselle.' Neither of their faces moved. 'He came over from Texas, a private investigator, like me.'

I recounted how Brasselle had contacted Angela Procter, although I didn't use her name, referring to her simply as a member of the staff of Ad-Hoc. Apart from that, the story was as I knew it, about the missing file, the red star system, and so forth. They were interested when I reported how upset Jeff Stone had been, but didn't interrupt.

'After that, the lady got worried about what she was doing. She didn't mind breaking a couple of rules, if it would help this orphan child in Texas, but she didn't want to break any laws. She came to see me, get my advice. I thought the first thing to do would be to check out this Brasselle, so I came here to have a talk with him. Somebody else got here first. The man was already dead.'

'What a nasty surprise,' commented Cohen.

'You must have been terrified,' supplemented his stable-companion. 'What explanation did you give the police?'

They probably knew already that I didn't blow the whistle. Even if they didn't, they

146

would soon find out. I shook my head.

'I didn't call them.Almost as soon as I found him, I heard the sirens outside.'

'So they found you here?'

'No. There was nothing I could tell them. I beat it out the back way, as they came up the stairs.'

'Tut tut,' reproved Fisher. 'Not the kind of thing I'd expect to hear from an honest citizen.'

I shrugged.

'Like I said, there was no way I could help. Being in the business I am puts me in a different category from the average rubberneck. Those guys would have put me in the slammer automatically as a material witness. It hampers a man's activity, that kind of thing.'

'But you were entirely innocent,' protested Cohen. 'Why should they do such a thing?'

My smile was not forced.

'Your people are so involved with international spy-rings, conspiracies and the like, you're out of touch with the working world. It's a hot sweaty day in summer. You're a hot sweaty cop in an understaffed department, with more beefs on your hands than any one man can handle. Suddenly, there's an extra murder tossed in your lap, and what do you find? A man with a gun. What kind of man? Another policeman? Someone from the D.A.'s office? Even the city dogcatcher? No. A private investigator, an object of natural suspicion at all times. You don't have time to waste with a lot of questions, and checking and stuff like that. You heave him in the can. And that's exactly what would have happened to me.'

They exchanged amused glances.

'Friend Preston is something of a cynic, wouldn't you say, George?'

'World-weary,' agreed George. 'Do we believe him?'

'Let's defer that for now. Get on with the story, Preston. You ran away from the police, like any innocent man would. Then what?'

'I reported back to my client, suggested we both keep out of it. Then there was a phone-call to my office—'

'—oh, you have an office?'

'—and a secretary too. She took the call. It was from a man named Hubbard. The manager of this place. I'd seen him when I first came here, and he remembered me. For reasons of his own, he kept quiet about me when he was talking to the police. He wanted to see me. I met him this afternoon. He said he had information to sell. Wanted ten thousand dollars for it. If I didn't buy, he knew someone else who would.'

'Who?' interjected Cohen.

'He didn't say who.'

'But who did you think it might be?' persisted Fisher.

148

'I hadn't the faintest idea, then or now. I told him I didn't know whether I could raise the money. He gave me till ten o'clock tonight. And here I am.'

'Yes, here you are. Why?'

'To hear what he's selling.'

'Why would you care? Or your client, for that matter? This mysterious female client. Nothing you've said so far would justify giving that kind of money to a blackmailer.'

To Fisher's surprise, I agreed with him.

'You got it right,' I told him. 'That was almost exactly what I said to—to this woman. Keep out of it. Let the law handle it. That kind of thing.'

'Very commendable,' said George Cohen drily.

'But you're still here,' Fisher pointed out.

'And with the money.'

I tried to turn it into a between-us-men situation.

'My client is a very wealthy lady. The money won't hurt her credit one little bit. She's excited about all this. Excited, and very curious. You know how women are, if they get the track of a mystery. Gus Brasselle had the name of a woman among his stuff. Iris Moorland. My client's husband was badly hurt in an automobile accident eighteen months ago. The Moorland woman was driving the car that hit him. That's a far cry from an orphan child in Texas, and it doesn't fit. It doesn't jell

149

with any of the rest of what he told her.'

Cohen nodded wisely.

'Ah yes. Iris Moorland, didn't you say? What did you make of it?'

'Damned if I know. But I think this Brasselle had a lot more going than he was telling my client. There's one extraordinary coincidence. My client has access to the records at Ad-Hoc. The Moorland woman has access to the medical records at the County Hospital. The man she ran over was what you might call a founder member of Ad-Hoc.'

'And what does he make of it, your client's husband?'

This from Fisher.

'I wish I could ask him. The poor guy is a zombie. The accident damaged his brain.'

'So we're talking about Doctor Edwin Proctor,' nodded Fisher.

'And your client is his wife, Angela,' added Cohen.

I don't know why I should have been surprised.

'You people are ahead of me,' I accused.

'Only most of the time,' corrected Fisher. 'There's still a lot we don't know. Have you talked with her, the Moorland woman?'

'No, I haven't. I had a man check her out. Routine stuff. Style of living, credit status, that kind of stuff. She has a clean bill.'

Cohen's face was a study in disbelief.

'And that's all the interest you took? Either

you're not very efficient, or we're not getting the whole story.'

Trying to keep my voice calm, I said,

'I didn't know the connection with Doctor Proctor until less than one hour ago. Until then, all I had on Iris Moorland was that she's a hard-working, keep-my-nose-clean kind of woman, whose life consists of her job and her child.'

'Ah yes. The child,' agreed Fisher. 'Nice little thing. Sweet disposition.'

'I wouldn't know.'

'A credit to her mother,' Cohen assured me.

'Her adoptive mother,' his partner added. 'Little Kim Moorland was a shipmate of your Texas orphan's. They came over together. On the good old Newland Hope. Quite a coincidence, wouldn't you say?'

I absorbed this new information, thinking rapidly.

'No, I wouldn't,' I said slowly. 'I would say it was a hell of a lot more than a coincidence. But I still don't know what it means.'

George Cohen pointed a finger at me.

'Maybe I can help. Try this. Suppose Edwin Proctor found something, some medical record or whatever, that made him suspicious about the clearance procedures for the orphan children coming through the Ad-Hoc organisation. He begins asking questions. Before he comes up with answers, he has an unfortunate accident. A long time later,

151

another man begins asking the same kind of questions. Somebody kills him.'

They both looked at me expectantly.

'I would say those records might have something to say. And here's another one for you. Angela Proctor also asked questions today. Tonight, while I was talking to her, somebody took a shot at us, with a rifle. It would all seem to go together, wouldn't it?'

'Yes, it would.'

It was Cohen who spoke. The man from the Maritime Commission, I recalled. Something slotted into place.

'I'm just beginning to see where you fit in, Mr. Cohen. You're not checking on some homicide case. All this end of it, my end of it, is incidental. Just detail. You're investigating the Newland Hope disaster. But why now? Why so late in the day?'

He snorted in disgust.

'Late in the day,' he echoed. 'I think I'm going to tell him, John.'

'Very well. He could be useful to us, so he might as well know what he's getting into.'

It's always a comfort to know you're going to be used.

CHAPTER ELEVEN

'I'm going to skip over most of it,' Cohen began. 'Just stick to the few essentials. The Newland Hope caught fire a few miles offshore, with eighteen hundred infant immigrants aboard. It could have been a much bigger disaster than it was. Fortunately, the fires were brought under control. That was a big bonus. In addition, the local yacht club went out in force, to bring the children ashore.'

I'd heard this already from Angie, but it wouldn't pay me to seem too knowledgeable. So I asked the obvious question.

'Why? I mean, if they were beating the fire—'

'Smoke,' he explained tersely. 'The babies would have died from the smoke. It must have been a hell of a scene out there, with the fire, and the small boats alongside trying to disembark these children. Overall, it was a big success. But there were casualties. One of the larger launches was lost, on the return journey. We think it must have damaged itself against the side of the mother ship, and foundered at speed. All hands were lost. You probably read it at the time. At the end of the operation, there were almost two hundred of those children lost. That's why it's classified as a

153

disaster. But we have to bear in mind that over sixteen hundred were saved.'

He paused, as if expecting comment.

'Yes, I remember all that. There was a big ceremony for those lost at sea.'

'Correct. The bodies, of course, were never recovered. The currents out there would see to that. And it is shark fishing territory, as you may already know.'

I didn't care to let my mind dwell on the implications of that piece of information.

'I'm still listening.'

'The ship's captain was too drunk to take charge. After a lot of hearings, he was found guilty of dereliction of duty, gross neglect, a dozen charges. He committed suicide after the verdict.' The man from the Maritime Commission was speaking now in a flat, emotionless tone, not unlike the mechanical reproduction of a talking computer. 'The other major enquiry established that the fires on the ship were the result of sabotage. A man had gone missing the day she docked, one of the stewards. Such evidence as there was pointed to that man. As I say, he disappeared, and we never did find him. Not until two weeks ago. Then a man got fighting drunk over in Baltimore, and started talking about the Newland Hope. Fortunately, there was a police officer involved who thought the man might be holding some useful information. He was right, too. It was our missing saboteur, after all that time. He was handed over to my department, and we began to get the story. Somebody paid him five thousand dollars. He had two jobs to do. One was to dope the skipper. That wasn't too difficult, all he had to do was get access to the man's dinner tray. The other was to start those fires, in different parts of the ships, at a given time.'

There were a dozen questions bursting to get out of me, but the main one made it first.

'Why? I mean it wasn't an insurance swindle, there wasn't any cargo—'

I stopped, because the other two were shaking their heads.

'Wrong,' corrected Fisher. 'There was one hell of a cargo. Do you have any idea of how much money people in this country will pay for a baby?'

A baby. My mind began chasing down this new channel.

'No,' I admitted.

Fisher nodded, as though the answer was expected.

'It's difficult to be accurate. I mean they don't appear in the For Sale columns. But our best information is that a middle-aged childless couple, who for one reason or another have been unable to adopt a child through the normal adoption channels, will go as high as twenty-five thousand dollars. Maybe more, we can't be absolutely sure.'

It had been a long day. Maybe otherwise I

would have cottoned on a little faster.

'Are you saying this sailor stole one of those children, and smuggled it ashore?'

'No, he's not,' snapped Cohen irritably. 'He's saying somebody went to all that trouble to steal the whole two hundred. Two hundred babies, Preston.'

'At twenty-five thousand dollars apiece,' added Fisher.

'That's five million dollars. Five million.'

Cohen repeated the amount, rolling it around his tongue.

I blinked. 'Wow.'

'Wow, indeed. So now, you finally begin to get the picture.'

The magnitude of the operation was staggering. Even so, I still had objections.

'But the scale of the thing, that has to be self defeating, surely? I mean, if you want to bust into a jewellery store, there's no problem recruiting a couple of guys to help out. After a time, if you know the right people, you begin to unload the stuff. But babies? You don't just toss 'em into the back of a car, and drive away. Babies have to have food, attention, hygienic surroundings.'

Even as the thoughts turned into words, my voice was beginning to trail away.

Fisher wagged his head.

'I can see from your face that it's getting through. What you're saying is, to pull off a stunt that big, you have to have big

156

organisation. And guess who was already swinging into action before the first of those rescue boats hit the shore?'

'Ad-Hoc,' I muttered.

'Right.'

'Yes, but Ad-Hoc is a big outfit. In good standing. The kind of operation you're suggesting, would involve doctors, nurses, trained volunteers. The whole thing would have to be a massive conspiracy. I'm sorry if the thought processes aren't fast enough, but I'm just not finding it easy to absorb.'

''s O.K.' Cohen assured me. 'That was my own reaction at first. When you go into detail, it gets simpler. Your department, really John.'

Fisher explained.

'These people you mentioned, they are in the human life business. A baby needs a shot, he gets it. If it's formula time, they give it to him. They don't look at pieces of paper, they don't count numbers. If a baby is hungry, they don't demand to see his documents. They feed him. All that other stuff, the paperwork, that's for the administration people. And one man can handle a helluva lot of papers. You have to imagine the scene that night. It was dark, people working under emergency lighting, an atmosphere of crisis. Everybody dealing with the unexpected. Except for a handful of them. A small group of people, who knew in advance what was going to happen. They knew exactly what they were doing, had the arrangements

157

already in hand. With proper preparation, their job wasn't too difficult at all. We don't have all the details yet, but now we know the picture, they will follow. Are you sure you've told us all you know?'

I searched around in my mind. Apart from avoiding any reference to Mr. Shoemaker, I'd played very straight with these people.

'Yes,' I assured him.

'And there's no one else involved? No one you've taken into your confidence? What about this secretary you mentioned?'

'Florence? No. All she has is Hubbard's name. She has no idea what I'm working on.'

Cohen decided he'd been quiet long enough.

'So that leaves Mrs. Proctor. Where is she now?'

'At my place.' I hoped it would still be true. 'I told her to keep the door locked until I got back.'

He nodded.

'I would say that wraps it for now, John. We'd better get over there, and pick the lady up. What about Mr. Preston? You think he's told us all he knows?'

Fisher beamed.

'I would think so. There's only himself and the lady in this. We have all we need to clean it up.'

Clean it up? I didn't understand.

'Do you want to take care of him?'

'Not my turn,' protested Fisher. 'I just took care of Hubbard.'

Phonies. And I'd told them all I knew. I was in trouble, and I jumped to my feet. Cohen chuckled.

'I think he's getting the idea.'

'Bit late, old man.'

For a large man, Fisher was very quick in unsprawling, and facing me across the room. I had no chance against the two of them, both armed, and I cursed myself for being fooled the way I had.

There was a sudden heavy banging at the door.

'Police. Open up.'

The other two froze. I ran headlong at the window, folded my arms across my face, and dived through it. There was a crunch of splitting glass, pain at my shoulders and back, and I was falling into an alleyway at the side of the building. Somewhere behind me, a gun went off. Scrambling to my feet, I began to run towards the far end of the block. I emerged close to the rear entrance of the apartment building. A car stood at the kerb. I stared wildly at the man leaning on the bonnet. Behind me a voice said,

'In the car, Preston. Quick.'

To add point, something hard jabbed at my side. The car door stood open. Al Tuscano waved me in. I realised the man with the gun was brother Tony. I hesitated, and a firm hand sent me sprawling forwards.

'Lie down on the floor,' commanded Al. 'Stay there, if you don't want the cops to pick us all up.'

My nose was pressed against oily carpet. The car started, and we moved slowly away. After a few seconds, the movement stopped. A door banged, as someone else climbed inside. Then we were off again. From the front seat, a voice said,

'O.K. to get up now, Preston. Just sit quiet and don't start nothing.'

I pulled myself up onto the rear seat, next to an unsmiling Al. The two heads in front belonged to his brothers, George and Tony. Tony was at the wheel.

'Where to?' he queried.

'Somewhere off the street,' growled George. 'Anywhere.'

'Drive-in movie?'

'O.K.'

I seemed to be bleeding from a dozen places, where the shattered glass of the window had cut at me on my way through.

'You're in kind of a mess, ain't you?' grinned Al. 'It's that window trick. That'll do it, every time.'

'They'll never replace doors,' agreed Tony, happily.

My mind was in a turmoil, trying to adjust to this new situation. It didn't seem to be my night. I'd escaped by the skin of my teeth from

Fisher and Cohen. At the same time, I'd avoided being picked up by the police. Only to walk slap bang into these three characters. Somewhere, I wasn't doing it right. There was one thing I liked, though. Ordinarily, I stay away from drive-in movies, but tonight I was happy to be going. If these characters had any plans for me, such as liquidation, they wouldn't be doing it in a public place. So, for the immediate future, I didn't seem to have any reason to be afraid.

'Where did you guys come from?' I queried. 'And what do you want with me?'

George slewed his head around, and stared at me.

'For an escaped desperado, you're kind of pushy, it strikes me.'

'Right,' agreed Al. 'You should just be grateful you're out of it.'

That wasn't going to quiet me down.

'I'm not so interested in what I was got out of,' I told him. 'I'm more concerned about what I've got into.'

'Did you check the artillery, Al?' asked the eldest brother.

A swift hand patted at me.

'He's clean. Don't tell me you don't have iron, Preston. How come you're not wearing any?'

'A nasty man took it away from me,' I snapped.

'Heh, heh,' twitted Al. 'And you so tough

161

and all. How come you let him do that?'

'Because he told me he was a a G-man.'

George swung round again.

'A federal?' he demanded edgily. 'Are you saying the federals are mixing in this? Whatever it is?'

His brothers were listening hard now, and the grin had disappeared from Al's face. I liked George's last remark. It sounded as though these three were working in the dark, like me. That was good. On the other hand, why were they involving themselves at all? The answer to that one might be not too good. For me. They were still waiting.

'Not this time,' I denied. 'They both had genuine identification, or so it seemed. But they were phonies.'

'They?' queried Al.

'There were two of them. Look, why don't we leave this until we get to the movie?'

George faced front again, and there was silence. It would take a couple of minutes to get where we were heading, time for me to put my thoughts together. The two not-from-Washington men had been waiting when I reached the Granville Apartments. From the sound of things, they had already killed Hubbard. The point was, how did they get there? The only explanation I could muster was that Hubbard had jumped the gun, and contacted the opposition earlier than he'd promised. Instead of bringing money, they

162

brought his death sentence. He was nobody's hero material, and it wouldn't have taken the visitors long to find out that someone else was expected, the someone being me. They had been no ordinary gunmen, those two. They hadn't been sent out merely to kill Hubbard. Their job must have been to find out the extent of the interference, and clean it up. That would account for them having told me as much as they did. It was a cards-on-the-table session, the purpose being to find out how much I knew, and who else was involved. It didn't matter how much they revealed, because I would not be alive at the end to repeat it. The purpose had been to get me to talk. And how I talked, I reflected bitterly. I'd told them everything there was to know, with the one exception of Mr. Shoemaker's involvement. What I'd been doing was to lay Angela Proctor's life on the line. The thought made me go cold. If the police hadn't arrived when they did, I would be in the broom cupboard alongside the unfortunate Hubbard, and those two would be out after Angela.

The car slowed down as Tony Tuscano made a wide left turn into the movie-lot. In the distance, the vast screen was filled with dust, as an escaping waggon hurtled down a steep slope, with grim-faced Apaches in close pursuit.

'Not too close in Tony,' grunted George. 'I've already seen this one.'

'Me too,' chimed Al. 'Besides, we don't want all that dust over the car.'

Al was evidently the one with the shafting wit. The car stopped. For a moment there was silence. Then George said,

'All right, Preston, we're here. Talk it up.'

CHAPTER TWELVE

It was stuffy in the car. The hot, oppressive night was close around us. Dull pain throbbed at me from half a dozen cuts. I began to feel dizzy.

'Open some windows,' I croaked.

'Quit stalling,' said Al nastily.

I turned my head towards where his face floated, unsupported, a few inches away. It was all so unimportant. Why did everybody make such a great razza out of everything? A murder or two, here and there. A couple of hundred missing babies. What did any of it matter, when you stacked it up against a long, refreshing sleep? People have no sense of proportion these days. Al's face bobbed away. I slid forward, my chin banging against padded upholstery on the way down into the cool darkness.

'Passed out,' grunted a voice.

There was movement and noise. None of it seemed to be any of my concern. I liked it where I was, drifting in a disembodied half-world of my own. A strange sensation came into my feet, along with a scraping sound. Then a lot of light, and people hauling at my arms and shoulders. A pungent, acrid smell attacked my nostrils, and I jerked away from it.

'He's coming round.'

The smell again. One eyelid opened reluctantly.

'What'd I tell you? Never fails.'

I seemed to be sitting upright. What I wanted was to lie down. I rolled sideways, but an arm held me, and the smell was back, forcing tears.

'No you don't, champ.'

'That's right,' agreed somebody. 'You'll take him in the next round.'

This time I took a proper look. A wood-walled room, with too much lighting for my taste. The Tuscanos were scattered around in chairs, watching me. A small, wizened face nodded encouragingly. I'd seen it before. Yes. A waiter at Buck's Rancho. He didn't look much like a waiter now, with his medical supplies laid neatly beside him on the floor. He was busy pressing adhesive tape into position on my side. Somewhere along the line I seemed to have lost my jacket and shirt. I licked at dry lips.

'Here.'

A glass was thrust under my nose.

'Don't gulp it. Kind of swill it around inside

165

your mouth, and then swallow. One mouthful is all.'

The little man spoke with authority. I did it his way. The cold liquid was good.

'You're doing fine,' he encouraged. 'Guess he's O.K. now, boss.'

'A nice job you did Walter,' approved George. 'You through with him now?'

'I guess,' nodded Walter. 'But he shouldn't oughta try for no title shots tonight.'

He went away, and I was sorry. I was beginning to like the little guy. I called after him,

'Thanks, Walter.'

At the doorway, he turned, grinning.

'You bet.'

There was a scattering of adhesive tape around the upper half of me, as though I'd been acting as a model for trainee first-aid students. But there was no more blood, and the aching was dulled. Walter hadn't spent his whole life waiting on tables. I moved my arms gingerly, and was gratified at the absence of pain.

'Walter seems to know his business,' I grunted.

'He was ten years in the fight game,' explained Tony. 'Glue 'em together and push 'em back in the ring.'

'But we don't have a bell, so don't come out fighting. We're not in the mood,' advised Al.

My mind was clearer now, clear enough to

make me wonder what these characters wanted with me. It wasn't straightforward violence, that much was clear. They could have done anything they wanted with me from that first moment after I sailed through the window.

'All right, Preston, you stalled us long enough. Where is Mrs. Proctor?'

George Tuscano leaned his elbows on the small table in front of him, and stared at me hard through wreathing cigar smoke.

Angie. I looked at my watch. It had been almost two hours since I left her back at Parkside, with instructions not to move for one hour. She hadn't wanted to make that agreement in the first place. The chances of her exceeding the time limit were thin.

'I don't know,' I replied. 'And why should I tell you, even supposing I did?'

If only I knew where these brothers fitted into the picture. It was a fairly safe bet they were not on the same team as my two non-government buddies from Hubbard's apartment. That being so, it seemed unlikely they were part of the baby-snatching set-up. What then? What else was there?

'Don't start getting tough,' pleaded George. 'You'll be scaring my little brothers here.'

'That's right,' agreed Al. 'He's making me nervous already.'

When in doubt, charge. I read that in some old cavalry manual one time.

167

'Some people already tried to kill me tonight,' I said evenly. 'They wanted to know where Angie Proctor was, too. It seems to me that lady is in a lot of trouble. And I don't like the kind of people who are trying to find her. I didn't like them, and I don't like you. Go to hell.'

Al was halfway out of his chair, face working.

'Listen you—'

'Siddown,' barked George.

'Nobody talks to me—'

'Siddown.'

Al Tuscano glared at his brother, black anger radiating from him. But he sat down. I relaxed, thankfully. Walter had been right. I was in no shape for a crack at the title. George looked at me thoughtfully.

'There's three of us here. Plenty more outside. I don't have to draw you no pictures. So what's with all the grandstand? Are you stuck on that lady?'

I'd wondered that briefly myself.

'No,' I denied. 'But she hired me. Suddenly, half the town is looking for her. If she's in some kind of trouble, I guess I have to be on her side. That's it.'

I put on a determined look, and stared him out.

'You think we want to hurt her?'

'It seems possible,' I said stonily. 'It's a cinch you don't want to take her to the graduation

168

ball.'

'Teh heh.'

Tony chuckled with delight, and came over to me.

'Here, have a cigarette. We don't have a blindfold.'

The smoke was good, and I nodded my thanks.

'You got us all wrong, Preston. You couldn't be more wrong.' George pointed his cigar at me. 'Is that on the level, about she hired you for something?'

'Absolutely.'

'Talk about the something,' he encouraged.

On the point of refusing, I paused, and looked around. These people meant business, and their business seemed to include worrying about Angela Proctor. There's nothing heroic about a one-man crusade, if the one man turns away from possible help.

'There was a man from Texas, by the name of Brasselle,' I began.

I told them about the pitch he had given Angie Procter, and the way she became concerned over his insistence, and so she hired me to check him over. Somebody killed him, and that led me on to the rest of the big story, the Newland Hope disaster. They all listened with great care. I only told them those things that would make a consecutive story. It didn't seem necessary to burden them with any ideas I may have picked up along the way. And Mr.

169

Shoemaker was never referred to at all.

Brother George breathed heavily, and an inch of cigar-ash fell unheeded to the floor.

'Two things don't make sense,' he objected. 'First off, why are you telling us all this?'

'Because I'm tired, George,' I told him wearily. 'And I don't have any inclination to sit around watching you people tear off my ears.'

Tony said ho-ho, and slapped his knee.

'You gotta admit, the guy can figure.'

'Quiet Tony,' remonstrated the senior brother. 'But suppose it's us, just suppose it's us snatched all those kids. Then what?'

'Then I'm dead right now,' I said frankly. 'But I don't have you doing that. You see, whoever did that is against Mrs. Proctor. That much I know. And you're for Mrs. Proctor. That much I think I know.'

He nodded, absorbing this.

'Kay. The other thing that bothers me, is why she should pay out good money to hire you. A stranger. She knows we'll do anything for her.'

'Right,' agreed Al. 'And there's three of us. Answer the man, Preston.'

I shrugged.

'You'd have to ask her that one. Maybe she decided my approach would be a little more subtle. I'd ask questions. You'd probably wade in with baseball bats.'

Al snorted.

'I don't like it. It don't feel good. Why don't

170

we bounce him around the walls a little? He may change his story.'

George's reply was definite, and I looked at him gratefully.

'No,' he decided. 'I'm buying the story. If he's playing games with us, you can have him later. Right now we have to find Angie.'

Tony snapped his fingers.

'Heh, those guys back at the hotel. They'll be looking for her too.'

I woke up suddenly.

'Guys? You mean the imitation G-men? The police will have them.'

He shook the good-humored head.

'No. They came through the window, same as you. I saw them hit the dirt as we pulled out.'

George was on his feet and across the room like lightning. He grabbed the front of Tony's shirt and dragged him upright.

'Why the hell didn't you say so before?' he shouted.

Tony was shaken.

'I didn't know who they were then. Coulda been anybody. Our deal was to get Preston out of there. It just kind of fell into place.'

George swore, and let him go.

'They must have a thirty minute start,' he growled.

'A thirty minute start to where, George?' queried Al, and for once I could see his point. 'We don't know which way any of these people would go. Angie, the G-men, anybody.'

It was as though they'd forgotten me for the moment.

'I'll tell you one thing,' I offered. 'There are too many people now who know too many bits of this story. It's about to blow, and when it blows, this city, this whole state could crack wide open.'

They all looked puzzled.

'So?' shrugged Al.

'So there's one place full of evidence. Files, statements, letters. The people behind all this need that stuff, and they need it now. Tonight. You want to help Angela Proctor, make sure all that evidence stays where it is. Protecting her life is one thing. I think if you gave her the choice between that, and safeguarding those files, she'd go for the files.'

Tony and Al looked doubtful, but waited for George's decision. I could see he was impressed.

'They already tried to kill her once tonight, to stop her telling what she knows,' I pressed. 'What matters is that evidence.'

Al couldn't keep quiet any longer.

'I don't know, George,' he grumbled. 'It sounds to me like working for the cops.'

'No,' I jumped in. 'It's working for a bunch of little kids. Orphans.'

That seemed to decide George.

'This stuff,' he demanded. 'Where do we find it?'

'The Ad-Hoc office building.'

'You know the way?'

'You bet.'

I was crammed in the rear seat of a dark sedan, as we tore through the city streets. Tony was next to me, humming softly and with an excited glint in his eyes. George and Al were in front, with little Walter at the wheel.

'You think maybe somebody might give us an argument?' Tony asked hopefully.

'Maybe,' I grunted. 'I'd feel better dressed if I had a piece.'

He looked at me, nodded his head, then leaned forward to tap Al on the shoulder. They muttered to each other, then Tony turned back to me. He was holding out a black automatic.

'We'd like it back,' he grinned.

He was a man you felt you had to grin back at. I thought I'd risk a question.

'Look, don't get sore, and if you don't want to tell me, I'll mind my own business, but why are you men so strong for Angela Proctor?'

He stopped grinning for a moment, and I thought he was about to refuse me. Then he shrugged.

'Where's the harm? Angie's O.K. Kind of high-flown sometimes, but we keep an eye on her for Doctor Ed. That's her old man. He's sick, you know.'

I didn't understand yet.

'Yes, I heard about his accident. But I still

173

don't get it.'

'It was years ago, way up in San Francisco. Al and me was just squirts at the time. George was feeding us the best he could, because he was our ma and pa. He had to be, there wasn't nobody else. We got sick. Al and me, that is. George didn't have money for doctors. But Doctor Ed, he took care of us. Stayed with us three days straight, in that room we lived in. He wouldn't take a nickel then, and later, when we started to make a few bucks, he still wouldn't let us pay him. We would have died, there ain't no doubt about that. It ain't Angie you see, not really. It's for Doctor Ed.'

We avoided looking at each other after that.

The car was getting close to the Ad-Hoc building now.

'Make a left turn up ahead,' I called.

We made a wide sweep into the turn. George's voice sounded urgently.

'Kill the lights. Pull over.'

At once, Walter switched off the lights and braked as we scraped the kerb. We all stared into the darkness ahead.

'We got company,' announced George.

The moonlight was weak that night, obscured by a watery haze in the sky. As my pupils adjusted to the gloom I could make out the Ad-Hoc building a block ahead. Parked in front was a large flat-top furniture waggon. There were no lights in the building, except the security lighting at the street level. This was bright enough to enable us to distinguish the figures of men scuttling back and forth, carrying stuff out of the place and into waiting hands inside the truck.

'Looks like you called it, Preston,' muttered Al. 'What do we do, big brother?'

'One thing we can't do is to go in there blasting,' warned George. 'There's nine or ten of those guys that I counted already. Maybe more.'

Tony agreed.

'Yeah. On top of that, most of those people won't be opposition anyway. Just working stiffs doing a job.'

Al had an objection.

'You call that doing a job?' he queried. 'Shifting all these files and stuff that way? Hiding the evidence?'

Al had never shown up as the bright one of the trio. George explained, with heavy patience.

'They don't know they're doing that Al. All they're told is, they have to take the stuff from one place to another. It's just a job, like Tony says.'

But Al still thought he had a trump card.

'In the middle of the night?' he crowed.

'Especially in the middle of the night,' countered Tony. 'It's a city ordinance. All these business guys have to shift their stuff outside the working day. So they don't foul up the traffic.'

The middle brother grunted, and was silent. George had made up his mind.

'Tony, go call the cops.'

'Cops?'

Tony, Al and Walter the driver all spoke in horrified unison.

'What'll I say?' demanded Tony.

'Tell 'em the joint is being burgled,' was the terse reply.

'What good will that do? You can bet those removal guys have proper instructions and stuff.'

George sighed heavily, and half-turned so that he could see us all.

'What good it does is to put the law on the scene,' he explained. 'It'll take a few minutes for them to be satisfied everything is on the up and up. Meantime, we wander down there, see if we can spot any old friends. That's where you come in, Preston. Nobody's going to start anything with a prowl-car right outside the front door. And if they do, that's O.K. too. We'll have the whole damned police force crawling all over the joint.'

Al crowed.

'Hey, that's pretty good, Georgie. We let the law do the work, huh?'

George sighed, and I could understand it. Al must have been a great trial to him over the years.

'You waiting for change, Tony?' he demanded softly.

Without a word, Tony opened the door and slipped out into the night.

'We'll give him a coupla minutes, then we'll—Christ. Look at that.'

There was a sudden glow at the upper windows of the building, then a lick of orange flame.

'Let's go,' snapped George.

We all piled out and began running down the street. In the front of the building, men were shouting, and the transfer of the stuff to the truck suddenly doubled in tempo. It was as though somebody had flicked a movie projector over to fast speed. As we got close, I pulled at George's elbow.

'Well?' he demanded.

'Whatever we find in there,' I explained, 'it's what's in the truck that counts. Somebody should follow it, find out where all this stuff is being taken.'

'You're right. Walter.'

'Boss?'

'Get back to the car. No matter what happens here, you stay out of it. Stick with that delivery truck. Find out where it goes, and catch up with me later. This is important, Walter.'

He added the last words because of the disappointment which was written all over the little man's face.

'You got it, boss.'

When we reached the offices, the hurrying

sweating men ignored us. The fire was what mattered now. It had gained a big hold in a matter of seconds. Some of the upper windows had shattered, and the black billowing clouds poured out, with great tongues of yellow and orange flame flashing intermittently, like neon signs. The noise was loud.

'See anyone?' George shouted.

I studied the faces of the carrying squad.

'No. They're probably inside, directing things. We'll have to go in.'

Al waited impatiently, George looked doubtful.

'Why? It's a cinch they can't stay in there long. Why don't we just pick 'em up as they come out?'

I shook my head.

'Too late then. They'll be the last to come out. If there was somebody else in there, somebody they forgot to bring with them, we'd feel terrible at the funeral.'

'Angie?' he asked anxiously.

'It's only a thought,' I demurred. 'But I'm going in.'

'You got it. C'm on Al.'

A police wailer sounded, but everybody was too busy to pay it any attention. We ran in at the front door. Whoever started the fire knew his business. The upper floors were ablaze first, leaving the street level usable for that extra few minutes. Then the flooring would collapse, and the fire would drop through.

178

Inside, the air was a haze of dust and light smoke.

I knew the elevators would be out of action. The stairway seemed fire-free so far. As I dived for the stairs, Al grabbed my arm.

'Are you crazy? What are you looking for?'

'The stuff that matters is up there somewhere,' I told him.

He was not impressed.

'This is as far as I go. You suit yourself.'

George waved at him to search through the lower rooms. I took the stairs two at a time. One of my plasters jerked free, and there was tearing pain as the wound re-opened. As I rounded the first landing, a figure loomed ahead in the smoke. It was the man who passed himself off as George Cohen. I was at him before he recognised me. There wasn't time for a lot of ringcraft. I kicked him hard in the groin, caught him as he slumped forward, and threw him headlong down the stairs. Panting, I turned back, to see another man emerging through the dust. It was Fisher. He saw me at the same moment, and shouted, reaching in his pocket. I grabbed for the gun Tony had given me. He fired first, and someone passed a red-hot poker through my thigh. I was squeezing the trigger now, and he buckled at the knees, gun dropping from suddenly nerveless fingers. I hobbled past him. He made a half-hearted grab at me, but I kicked him in the shoulder, and he was finished.

Those two men hadn't been carrying anything away, so what had they been doing up here? I coughed my way along the way they had come, and came to a closed door. It wouldn't open, and then I realised there was a key on the outside. I turned it quickly, and practically fell inside. There was a figure stretched out on the floor. A man, I saw thankfully. I turned him over, and he groaned. Then he opened his eyes, and looked at me with fear.

'What's happening?' he queried feebly. 'Who're you?'

'The place is on fire. Can you walk?'

'I think so. Oh, my head. Somebody hit me.'

'Talk later,' I insisted. 'Let's just get out of here.'

I began to pull him towards the door. He protested.

'No wait. The records. They're stealing the records.'

'Let 'em,' I advised. 'If they were left here, they'd all be destroyed. Are you coming, or not?'

He was still half-dizzy from the blow on the head.

'Yes. Yes, of course.'

There was a crashing noise from the corridor outside. The ceilings were starting to collapse through. We didn't have many seconds to play with. I've seen the way fire spreads. In the corridor, I held a hand over my face, felt the skin begin to scorch.

'No, No,' protested the man. 'Have to go back.'

He actually turned in the doorway. I was going to have to sock him on the chin and carry him out. I drew back my arm. He shook his head wildly, pointing back inside.

'Angie,' he croaked.

I pushed him violently towards the staircase. 'Get out of here. I'll go back.'

The corridor carpet was alight now, and the creeping flames were moving steadily towards me. My thigh was hurting like hell, and I doubted whether I'd have the strength to drag Angie Proctor free. If she was there. The room was filling with smoke, and I groped around for her.

'Angie,' I shouted angrily. 'Angie. Answer me, damn you.'

It was useless. The room was empty. If I didn't want to wind up as the charred remains of an unidentified man it was time to leave. I got to the door before I heard the thumping. There was a cupboard standing against the wall. I opened the door, and Angela Proctor's terrified face stared at me.

'Mark. Oh, Mark.'

She flung out her arms, and fell against me, coughing.

'Up you come, baby. You have to help.'

Arms round each other, we coughed and

stumbled towards the stairs. The other man must have made it to the bottom. Angie gasped as she stumbled into Fisher, who was either unconscious or dead.

'Mark, we have to get him down.'

'Leave him,' I snarled. 'He left you, didn't he?'

She stared at me, amazed and angry.

'He's a human being. You take that arm and heave.'

I swear she'd have stayed with him if I'd refused. Reaching down on my good side, I got a grip under his shoulder, and we got him as far as the head of the stairs. There was a roaring and cracking sound, and a great chunk of blazing wood missed Angie by inches. I wasn't going to get fried for Fisher's benefit, and neither was she. Not if I could prevent it. I planted a foot square in the middle of his back and gave a mighty shove. He toppled forward, bumping and sliding down the stairs.

'Go down, or you'll get the same,' I rapped. I meant it, too. The strength was nearly all gone from me.

Her face was a study in loathing and fear. But she went down. Thankfully, I stumbled after her. At the bottom, George and Al Tuscano looked up in amazement at the spectacle of Fisher bouncing down the stairs like a rubber ball. Then Angie Proctor, scared half to death. Finally me, gripping the wall with each step.

'Outside,' decided George. 'Everybody out. This is no place for a meeting.'

The stairs behind me suddenly flared with light, and my suit was on fire. Al was across in a flash, wrapping his jacket around me tightly. Somehow, we all made it out to the street. A thin crowd had already gathered, and policemen were pushing them away from the entrance. The big furniture wagon was still parked. Walter bounced up, grinning.

'What with all the excitement, boss, I kind of let down the tyres.'

'You did fine, Walter,' replied George.

I beckoned Walter to me, and whispered in his ear.

'I got a gunshot wound in the thigh, Walter. Can you glue me together?'

He looked doubtful.

'Gunshot? Well, I don't know. There ought to be a doc here any minute—'

'Can't wait around. Take a look, huh?'

'All right. I'll help you down to the car.'

The fire on my jacket had been smothered by Al's prompt action. I handed him his coat back with a grin. He winked. A police officer saw Walt and me moving away, and said something to George.

'It's all right, officer. The man has been hurt. It's nothing serious. The doctor is just taking him to the car for emergency attention.'

'Not before time,' he grumbled.

He made me sit in the rear seat, and

climbed in beside me, clicking on the ceiling light.

'H'm,' he mused, poking painfully around. 'Must be your lucky day, friend. There's no lead in there. The slug was just passing through, as you might say.'

'Very funny. Can you glue it together?'

'Just for a few hours, is all. You really need a proper doc. I'll do what I can.'

I leaned thankfully back against the leather, while his expert fingers went to work. Now I had a chance to think.

It was over. At least, the hard part was over. The rough stuff. The records were saved, and in official hands. The rest would come later, the outcry, the public fury, the denials in high places. Because there had to be high places in this. The whole operation reeked of organisation on a large scale. Well, they could all get on with it now. It was too big for me. I was just a guy hired to tail another guy's daughter.

That reminded me. Angie was going to be in for some hard questions, and soon. The least I could do was to tip off her father.

'Do you have any change, Walt? I have to make a phone-call.'

CHAPTER THIRTEEN

When I got to the bank of elevators, they stood silently waiting, doors open. All but one. The small one at the end of the line. The only one that went as high as the penthouse suite. Above the doors, a soft amber light glowed behind the 'P'. I leaned on the button, and wondered. Seconds later, the satin-finished steel slid open, and I stepped inside. There was perfume in the air, a sensuous, lingering smell, and my nostrils enjoyed it during the brief upward flight. Then there was that gentle pinging sound, and I was staring out into that same carpeted hallway I'd seen last time. When had that been? A couple of days ago? A hundred years? Whatever the calendar had to say about it, it had been a long time in real terms. In terms of pain and suffering, personal torment. And death. That too. A lot of people had been through a lot of experience since I last stepped out of that elevator. And it wasn't over, I knew that. There were people all over the state, all over the nation for all I knew, tucked up in bed asleep. Safe. Or so they thought. One day, soon, or maybe not so soon, but inevitably, hard-faced men would be knocking on their doors. Their time of suffering would begin then.

The plain oak door stood open, and I

remembered that on the last visit, the son Andrew had told me that the arrival of the elevator sounded the chimes automatically. I took one final appreciative sniff at the perfume and stepped out. No one came to the door, so I banged on it with my fist.

'It's me, Preston,' I called out.

Somewhere inside, a woman screamed. There was the loud report of a gunshot. Then a flat, cracking sound, and a crash. I was already running when I heard the crash. When I got to the huge reception room, I didn't see anything at first. The lights were blazing, and the place seemed deserted. Then there was a groan, a man's voice. In a far corner, Shoemaker stood up. He'd been kneeling on the floor, which was why I hadn't seen him.

'Mr. Shoemaker,' I called.

He shook himself, and peered around to locate the voice. In his hand was a heavy service revolver. It dangled at his side, as though it had no part of him.

'Preston?' he intoned abstractedly.

I walked over softly, not taking my eyes away from the gun. In front of him, on the floor, lay a woman. I'd never seen her before, and I didn't like the stillness of her face. Shoemaker took a pace back as I drew close.

'The gun,' I muttered, pointing.

He held it out without a word. I took it, sniffing at the barrel. An acrid odor stung my nose, and I stuck the gun in a side pocket.

Kneeling beside the woman, I saw the large black hole in her chest, with the sticky, red-rimmed edges. There wasn't any necessity for feeling pulses, or checking eyelids. She was dead the moment that heavy slug tore into her.

'I'll—I'll call a doctor.'

His voice was old, uncertain. Tremulous.

'The only thing a doctor can do is to sign a death certificate,' I told him. I made it as gentle as I could, but death is a hard fact.

'Dead,' he repeated, almost like a child. 'Are you saying she's dead?'

I scooped up a nickel-plated automatic that lay by the outflung hand of the dead woman. That had been fired too. Then I stood up, my mind in a state of confusion over this new development. Hadn't there been enough for one day? I felt something akin to an infantile resentment against the dead woman, whoever she might be. I was tired and irritable, and I'd lost a lot of blood earlier on. She didn't have any right to come around making more complications this way. Who was she anyway?

'Who was she anyway?' I repeated out loud.

He sank into a chair, an expression of total bewilderment on his face. Screwing up his eyes, he passed a hand over them and shook the handsome head. It was as though he'd forgotten I was there.

'My career,' he muttered brokenly.

I was just in time to head off the sharp retort that sprang to my lips.

'The woman,' I insisted. 'Who was she? What happened here?'

He looked across then forcing himself back to the present.

'I don't know.'

And that seemed to end it as far as he was concerned. But it wasn't going to be enough for the rest of the world.

'Look,' I said firmly. 'I don't know how much time we have. An hour if we're lucky, but it could be only minutes. You have to talk to me, and now. Before I call the police.'

That got through, first time around.

'Police? Oh no, we can't—that is—'

'Oh yes we can, and we do,' I assured him. 'You can't expect to hush up a thing like this. Fifty years ago you might have had an outside chance. Today, no chance at all. Let's get to it.'

He listened, with careful patience. Then he waved an arm towards the enormous, leather-topped desk beside him.

'I was waiting for you to come. You telephoned to say you were on your way.' He made it sound like an accusation.

'Fifteen minutes ago,' I confirmed.

'Just so. I'd been cleaning my revolver when you called—' there was a small bottle of oil and a stained rag resting on an old newspaper on top of the desk—'so I carried on with it. I heard the elevator arrive, and opened the front door so you could walk straight in. It had to be you, because no one else was expected.

188

Nobody else even knew I was here. I'm supposed to be playing poker with a few friends tonight.'

'So you went and opened the door,' I prompted.

'Oh no. I didn't go anywhere. There's a button behind the desk. The door opens electrically.'

It would.

'Go on.'

'The next thing I knew, this young woman came rushing in. She was in a terrible state of agitation. She began talking wildly, said that I had sent you after her to take her baby away. I tried to calm her down, because believe me she was in an advanced state of hysteria. I told her she was a stranger to me, and that I had no knowledge of her daughter, and would she please put away the gun she was holding. She was waving this gun about, did I mention that?'

I held up the automatic.

'This one?' He nodded. 'No, you didn't mention it before. Then what happened?'

'She began to rave about the government of this country. A lot of very confused, ideological stuff about the people taking over, and everyone like me being strung up and so forth. It was all very disjointed, and vague, as though she was quoting from half a dozen different agitators. There were all the familiar phrases, but there was no thread to it. I

189

stopped trying to reason with her, because every time I spoke, her face would start working, in a crazy way, and that gun would come pointing at me again. I'm not a man who frightens easily, Mr. Preston. But that woman frightened the hell out of me.'

I could tell that. His hands were still shaking.

'Then she said something I didn't understand at all. She mentioned her baby again, and this nonsense about my trying to take the child away. She became suddenly quiet, almost controlled, and I thought for a second the madness was passing. I couldn't have been more wrong. Her next remark chilled me more than anything she'd said so far. I wasn't the first one to attempt to steal her child. My son-in-law had tried, a long time ago. She fixed him, those were her actual words. She fixed him, by running him down with her automobile.'

He looked across to see if I understood him.

'I know about Doctor Proctor,' I said. 'And I know about the accident. Iris Moorland.'

'Who?'

'Moorland,' I repeated. 'Iris Moorland. That was the name of the woman driving the car.'

'I didn't recall the name. It was almost two years ago. So that must be—?'

He indicated the dead woman. I nodded.

'It has to be. We can soon find out. Please

finish the story first.'

He nodded abstractedly.

'No sooner had she told me about poor Edwin, than the chimes rang again. This time it had to be you. I was never so relieved in my life. She realised at once that someone was coming in, and it sent her entirely to pieces. She let out a horrible scream, and fired at me. As it happened, she missed, but that was an automatic pistol she was using, and there were plenty of other cartridges to come. My own gun lay by my hand. I—I can only guess it was entirely a reflex action. God knows I wished her no harm. But I grabbed the revolver, and fired back. Then you came in.'

'And that's everything that happened?'

'Everything.'

I knelt down beside the body. A black leather purse was half-trapped beneath her, and I had to push at her shoulder to free it. Shoemaker watched without much interest as I rummaged around inside. It was the usual collection of junk. Half-finished lipsticks, a pack of cigarets, some small change and a few bills tucked in a side compartment. A hand-mirror, a comb, a box of eye liner, two handkerchiefs. One stick of cologne, a pocket diary. The diary announced that it was the property of Iris Sheila Moorland, 2426 New Monastery Drive. There was a photograph inside. I looked at the smiling face that had once belonged to the woman on the floor, and the chubby baby who was staring at the camera in some alarm. Everything smelled of that generalised perfume, which comes from long mixing half a dozen different sweet odors. There was other stuff in the purse, but I'd seen all I needed.

I got to my feet, nodding.

'Iris Moorland,' I confirmed. 'Now it fits.'

'God, what a mess.'

Shoemaker buried his face in his hands. Sleep-waves washed at the back of my eyes. I blinked, shaking my head. It was no time to be dozing. There was a decanter on the desk, and a couple of glasses, one half-filled. I went to pour a drink into the empty one. As I raised it to my lips I saw a smear of lipstick on the rim, but it was no time to be getting squeamish. The liquor bit at the roof of my mouth, then my throat, spreading its rosy glow all the way down. I felt better. Physically.

'I came up here to report to you,' I told the shrunken figure opposite. 'But I guess that's been overtaken, as they say, by events.'

He looked up then.

'You'd better tell me everything,' he replied. 'There won't be an opportunity after—after the police get here.'

'The police? Oh, yes. Them. You were right to be concerned about what Angela was up to. She was starting to get on the track of something big. You remember the Newland Hope disaster? The ship with the immigrant children?'

'Ship? Yes. Yes, of course. A terrible business. Something like two hundred of them were lost, I believe. I don't see—'

'It gets clearer,' I cut in. 'The actual figure was two hundred and twenty three. But they weren't all lost. The actual number of bodies found was sixteen.'

He looked puzzled.

'Yes. The rest were lost at sea, if I remember.'

'No. Let me tell you what Angela was beginning to learn, and what I've been getting my nose into ever since you hired me.'

I sketched out the events of the past couple of days, right up until the time I walked out of the elevator.

'And there it is,' I concluded. 'There's an important string-puller behind all this. Somebody big, with flair and imagination as well as influence. You don't get a thing like this off the ground with the kind of talent that robs corner liquor-stores. It has to be someone with position and authority. I thought if I tipped you off fast enough, you'd be able to swing some high-powered action of your own, before the guy had a chance to cover his tracks.'

Some life returned to his face.

'Yes. That was good thinking. I shall still be able to do that, of course. This other business,' and he waved in the general direction of

Iris Moorland, 'that needn't hold up the investigation. I shall only need to make a couple of phone calls.'

He began to get up from the chair.

'No phone calls,' I snapped.

Shoemaker stared at me, uncomprehending.

'I don't think—'

'No phone calls,' I repeated. 'This Mister Big I was talking about, he already knows the whole story. He's one jump ahead the whole time. He can scarcely avoid it, with me telling him every detail.'

'You'll have to explain that,' he said stiffly. 'Do you mean you've been working for both sides?'

'I guess that's true in a way,' I replied bitterly. 'I've been acting the chump right along, without knowing it. If it hadn't been for this unfortunate woman here, I might not have twigged until it was too late.' I laughed sourly, a thin croaking noise. 'In fact, I might even have got dead myself. Tomorrow, the next day.'

Some of the haggard look was disappearing from his face.

'Go on.'

'She didn't come here to kill you,' I said, in flat tones. 'She came here for help. To ask you what the next move ought to be. You must have been having a drink, and talking about it, when you got my call. That changed your thinking fast.'

194

'Do you know what you're saying?'

'Oh yes. Finally. Finally, I do know what I'm saying. This glass, it has lipstick on it. The lady isn't wearing gloves, so there'll probably be fingerprints, too.'

'Nonsense. Circumstantial nonsense.'

I agreed with him.

'An expensive lawyer could talk his way round that one. Then there's the gun.' I showed him the automatic. 'You said she was waving this around. But she couldn't walk around the streets doing that. Couldn't drive a car, or even sit in a cab holding it. It had to be in her purse.'

'What of it?'

I sniffed at the gun, shaking my head.

'No perfume, no smell at all, except metal and a whiff of oil.'

Shoemaker snorted.

'You're snatching at snowflakes,' he sneered. 'Perhaps she had the gun in a pocket.'

'Look at her coat,' I invited. 'No pockets. She didn't have the gun at all. You put it by her hand after you killed her.'

The man was recovering his composure all the time now. If he'd ever really lost it. If all the earlier demonstrations had been anything more than a fine display of acting, for my benefit.

'I don't know your reasons for attempting to frame me in this way, but you will live to regret it,' he assured me. 'I can only think my

195

enemies must be paying you a great deal of money.'

He was good. He was very good indeed. I told him so.

'Bravo, Mr. Shoemaker. We're getting the politician now. The people's choice, huh? You know, until I came here tonight, I'd have probably voted for you myself.'

'I don't give a damn who you vote for,' he barked. 'Get the police, and let's have an end to this nonsense. They'll soon put paid to your fairy-tales.'

The trouble was, I tended to agree with him.

'Yes, I think they might,' I rejoined seriously. 'What with who you are, and who you know, and all those puppets you can jerk around, I don't need to be a genius to imagine you walking away from all this. They might even find something to charge me with. What would you guess? Defamation of character? That's always a good one.'

He was full of bounce again now, the platform manner screwed firmly in place.

'That, or one of a dozen other things. Monkey with me, Preston, and I'll see you ruined. Or worse.'

'Threats, yet.'

'And why not? I'm somebody in this town, in this State. In this whole country, dammit. Who do you think will listen to your grubby little accusations? You're nobody.'

I grinned. It was a very thin grin.

'I'll tell you what, though. I'm the kind of a nobody who knows guns. You said this woman took a shot at you, and you had to fire back, to protect yourself. You timed that one a second or two wide. You see, I heard those shots. The first shot was the heavy one, the one that killed your so-called attacker. The second shot was more of a cracking sound, the kind you get from an automatic. Wrong way around, Mr. Shoemaker.'

He shook his head.

'All nonsense. You'll have to do a lot better. Besides, you're overlooking your real weakness. I was the one who hired you in the first instance.'

'Yes, you did. I've been wondering about that, and I think I know the answer. Very few people will know of your involvement in this caper. Very few people, all very top level. The ones who do the work, carry out the orders, they wouldn't know about you. They wouldn't have any reason to connect Angela Proctor with their own top man, because they wouldn't know who he was. To them, she'd be just a dame who was getting too nosey. They might decide to do something about her, without your even knowing, until it was too late. So you put in your own man, to run interference. Me. I was to check on Angie, and report in. If it began to sound as if she was getting too close to something dangerous, you would be able to

197

prevent it. And if, in the process, I began to smell something, no problem. You would take me out. Just like that.'

'Madness,' he said, sadly.

'No. No, it isn't. Looking at it from your viewpoint, it's a simple matter of business prudence. You were probably surprised when your people knocked off Brasselle that way. I would even lay money you didn't know about him. What was he, anyway? F.B.I. ? Whatever it was, it didn't prevent your people getting rid of him. And that's what would have happened to your daughter, if she roamed around freelance. Hence me. And what a sucker I was. I told you everything that was happening. That's how you were able to put your goons on to poor little Hubbard. All he wanted was a few bucks.'

'A cheap, crawling blackmailer,' he retorted.

I nodded.

'He was that,' I admitted. 'But you've changed your tune.'

'Not really. It doesn't matter a damn what you say, or what you think. I'm too big for you, Preston. You lose.'

'Like Hubbard?'

'Exactly.'

'And the ship's captain, the one who killed himself over that disaster you created?'

'Only a weakling takes his own life,' he sneered.

'And the babies,' I persisted. 'Sixteen of

198

them died, either from the smoke, or in the sea. Were you too big for them, too?'

He waved me away impatiently.

'Statistics. Nothing more. Hundreds of them die every day out there. Thousands. What does it matter where they die?'

I shot him then. In the left shoulder. It rocked him back on the chair, and pain and rage fought for supremacy on his contorted face.

'I'll kill you for that,' he swore.

'No.'

My voice sounded like my thought. Far away. Detached. Then I heard myself speak again.

'What you said is probably true. You would get away with this. You're too big not to. I can't permit that. Reason I shot you in the shoulder is that it would give you time to grab for the revolver. Just the way you told me the story in the first place. Only you don't have the revolver any more. It's here, see.' I held it up. 'I figure you'd probably get off that one shot, the one that killed the woman. And at exactly the same moment she would loose a second shot at you. The one that killed you.'

There was no anger on his face now. Just fear. The fear of certain death.

'Preston, I'm a wealthy man—'

The voice didn't seem to notice.

'Somebody has to put it right. For the captain, you see. And for Gus Brasselle. All those little kids, the babies. Even poor old Hubbard.'

The automatic jumped once more in my hand. The slug went clean into his throat, and he died on a bubbling sound.

I wiped the gun clean of prints, then pressed it into the outstretched hand of Iris Moorland. Then I wiped off the revolver, forced his dead fingers around the butt, and dropped it to the floor.

Moving around, I cleaned off everything I'd touched, and went to the open door. The place smelled of cordite and death.

The carpet was a deep blue.

Odd, that.